FLAME CASTER

THE FIRE HEART CHRONICLES BOOK 2

JULIANA HAYGERT

COPYRIGHT

AUTHOR'S NOTE

DICTIONARY

Chey – daughter
Chini – son
Daj – mother
Dat – father
Gadjo – non-Romani person
Nais tuke – thank you
Ozi – fire
Phal – brother
Phen – sister
Puri Chey – granddaughter
Puri Chini – grandson
Puri Daj – grandmother
Puri Dat – grandfather
Rom Baro – leader of the enclave
Ruv – wolf/werewolf
Saint Sara-la-Kali – Romani Saint
Sastimos – a greeting
Vurdon – wagon

Yog – fire
Yog Ozi Nas – fire heart fever

1

I WAS ALWAYS A FIRM BELIEVER THAT EVERYTHING HAPPENED FOR a reason.

Now, for the life of me, I couldn't figure out why I was the Heart Maiden. I hadn't known I was a tzigane, a special kind of Romani with actual magical powers, until two months ago. I knew next to nothing about tzigane history and customs, even though the elder council *ordered* I studied it all ASAP. I had no control over my powers, and if it weren't for my mother's elixir, I would have killed a person or two by now.

I was also a hot-tempered, sharp-tongued, cut-the-bullshit kind of girl. I bet the council, with all their orders, would get tired of me fast.

But for now ... for now, I tried to compromise.

As I walked out of the classroom, my phone vibrated. I checked and it was a message from my mother.

Mom: *I'm 5 minutes late. Be there soon.*

Me: *Okay.*

Letting out a sigh, I exited the building and sat on the side of the stone steps. Students came and went; all of them went about their classes as if this were the real world.

If only I could still be that naïve.

Now I knew there was so much more to the world. There were magical creatures, there were monsters, and there were alchemists who were bent on using tzigane blood for terrible purposes. And they were after me.

That was why I wasn't walking to the bus stop. That was why I had to stay here, seated on this cold stone step, waiting for my mother to pick me up. Usually, she would be parked right in front of the building the moment I stepped out.

As much as I liked the break from being watched over twenty-four-seven, I hated staying put and doing nothing.

I pulled out my phone and found a text message from Ellie.

Ellie: *Hi, Mi. Raul wants to go to Muévete this Friday. Are you in?*

Shit.

Me: *I wish.*

Ellie: *Because of the alchemists?*

I had met Ellie about two months ago, when she started taking my flamenco classes at the dance studio I taught at. Even though I was quiet and wary of making friends, Ellie had broken through my walls, and soon I considered her my best friend. She had gotten a little creeped out when she found out I was a tzigane, but after the alchemists kidnapped us, she had come to terms with it. Mostly.

Me: *Yup.*

Ellie: *Then tell your hunky warriors to come with you.*

Me: *They won't go. I asked already, and they were vehement. They won't let me go anywhere like that anymore, and they won't take me.*

Ellie: *Jeez, that sucks.*

I agreed. Muévete was a great club about thirty minutes from Broken Hill that played lots of flamenco and reggaeton, which I loved. But since the alchemists' attacks, "my hunky warriors" and the elder council decided I couldn't go anywhere. There or any other clubs or bars, or anywhere that would make protecting me difficult.

Such a pain in my ass.

Ellie: *Is there anything I can do?*

Me: *Come and rescue me.*

Ellie: *Say when and where. I would love to teach the hunky warriors a lesson.*

I chuckled, imagining Ellie standing up to Artan and Theron, the two warriors who were always trailing me. I might pay to see that.

Letting out a sigh, I watched the road. Where was my mother? She was never this late.

A cold breeze blew by, and I tightened my suede jacket around me. The day was gray and dark for ten in the morning, but the forecast had called for clear skies in the afternoon, which would warm the day a little. But only a little since October in Connecticut was already too damn cold, in my opinion. I missed the heat of Florida.

Hmm, an idea popped in my mind. I bit my lip, wondering if I could pull it off. It would be a little risky with so many people walking by me, but I couldn't stop the little excitement filling my veins. What could I say? I liked risky and forbidden things.

I closed my eyes and focused on my magic. I called it from deep inside me. Because of the suppression elixir I drank every day, only a sliver answered. It was enough, though. I channeled it, coaxing it out of its hiding place.

Soon, the magic ran free inside me, and I let out a relieved exhale. At first, it had been odd to feel magic inside me. Now, it was a part of me. I pushed my magic under my skin, the fire in my magic, and focused on the heat, on the warmth.

Soon, my skin felt warmer, and I wasn't cold anymore.

A proud smile spread over my lips. I had done it. I had been able to warm myself with my magic, my *yog*—the tzigane word for fire.

But the heat kept increasing, kept coming, and my hands started turning orange.

Shit.

I closed my eyes again and focused. I pushed the magic back. I asked it to retreat, to let it go, before fire shot from my hands and everyone saw what I could do. Only the heat increased and panic took over.

Without thinking, I ran inside the building and into the nearest restroom. I turned on the cold water faucet and shoved my hands and arms under the water. A hiss echoed through the bathroom and a little smoke rose from my now damp jacket.

A girl stepped out from a stall and stared at my arms—and jacket—under the water.

"I ..." I started. But what could I say that made sense? Nothing came to mind. The girl looked at me as if I were crazy, then dashed out of the restroom without washing her hands.

I sighed.

When my magic was doused, I turned off the faucet and stripped off my jacket. Cursing, I folded the sleeves of my sweater to my elbows. Now I would be even colder outside. Damn, what the hell had I done?

It was only morning and my day was already going so well.

I dragged my feet back to the front of the building, fully expecting to see my mother parked in the fire lane, waiting for me, but to my surprise, she wasn't there.

Shivering, I picked up my phone and shot her a text.

Me: *Where are you? Everything okay?*

I stared at the phone, waiting for an answer.

The next set of classes was about to start. A large group of students rushed into the building. A guy bumped his shoulder into mine and I stumbled back.

He reached to me and held my upper arm. "Sorry."

A cold shiver rolled down my spine as I stared at him. He wore a black hoodie and a black mask over his nose and mouth. When I didn't answer, he humphed and continued his march to the building.

A long breath escaped my lungs, and I put a hand over my racing heart. Holy crap, what a scare. For a moment, I thought the guy was an alchemist, but his mask was a part of a scarf to cover his nose and mouth against the cold air. That didn't stop my overacting brain from imagining him conjuring a shadow dagger and piercing it into my heart.

I swallowed, trying to push those fears away.

The guy wasn't an alchemist. Not everyone who wore a hoodie, or a cloak, or a mask was an alchemist. I knew they could be hiding in plain sight like Phillip had done—he had pretended to be a normal human who liked me to get close—but after all I had been through, it was hard not to.

I shook my hand.

Mirella, stop.

I couldn't live in fear. I had to live as I always had. I refused to cower because of these damn alchemists.

And yet, when I saw my mother's car rounding the corner and coming toward me, I never felt more relieved.

I rushed down the steps, and once she stopped in front of the building, I jumped inside the car.

My mother, an older copy of me, knotted her brows. "What happened?"

"Nothing," I said, sinking into the seat.

She lifted an eyebrow at me. "Are you sure?"

"Yes. Just drive."

Without a word, she pulled away from the curb and back onto the road. "I've never seen you so eager to go to training."

"What can I say? I love getting my butt kicked." My voice dripped with sarcasm.

My mother shook her head, her eyes on the road.

I glanced at her as she drove. She asked what happened, but it wasn't as if she really wanted to talk to me. She never did. She wanted to be near me. She wanted to make sure I was all right, but talk? No. Every time I had tried to talk to her, she practically ran away. So why would I reach out to her when she never tried reaching out to me?

I crossed my arms and stared out the window, wishing time passed quickly and training wasn't so bad. At least, I would get to see Artan, even if the hunky warrior was always in a bad mood.

Maybe today, just today, he would be nice, or less horrible, and not kill me during training.

2

It all had been wishful thinking.

I landed on my butt with a gasp. Again.

Standing three feet from where I was sprawled on the floor, Artan shook his head. "You're not listening to me."

I groaned. We had been training for almost two hours. If I tallied all the hours he and Theron had spent teaching me to fight these past few weeks, it was probably more than my college and dance classes put together.

And yet, this fighting thing kept fighting me.

"I am listening," I complained as I pushed to my feet. My ass was sore, but I wasn't about to complain. "I already told you, I'm not cut out for this."

I brushed my hands on my thighs, trying to pretend it was dust from the floor, not the calluses that had been forming from working out too much. When I looked up, Artan's hazel eyes were fixed on me, on my legs, and his lips were pressed tight.

Heat spread through my cheeks.

I had caught him staring at me a few other times when we were training, and even though I didn't think he was really looking at me—no, just lost in thought—I couldn't help the flames licking my insides.

Artan cleared his throat and lifted his eyes to mine. "You have to be," he said, his voice rough. "Now, let's start over."

He took three steps back and positioned himself.

And then it was my turn to stare.

Artan's tall frame was clad in the warriors simple training clothes—light suede pants, a fitted Henley, and brown combat boots—and he stood with his powerful legs apart and fists raised. His biceps and shoulder muscles bulged. Even his face seemed sculpted out of perfect marble.

How could a girl be by his side several hours every day and not notice he was too handsome for his own good? How could she not feel attracted to him? I needed to know what magic that was, because damn, I wasn't sure I could resist much longer.

Thankfully, Artan was quiet and stoic and kept to himself. Besides the handful of times I caught him staring, there was no indication that he might be interested in me. Which was great. The thought of being rejected stopped me from making a fool of myself when things heated up—at least on my side. Each time he came closer and touched my hands and arms, showing me how to position them properly ... And once, when he actually stepped behind me and pressed his chest to my back, I had to ask for a break.

I probably needed one right now.

"I need some water," I muttered, turning from the center of the mat to the cubies along the wall.

My back turned to the fuming guy in the middle of the room. I took a long drink of my water. What did he expect from me? I was a dancer, not a fighter. Some of the kicks were okay, like roundhouse kick, but the position of the foot in a sidekick? Who the hell came up with that? My ballerina foot didn't twist that way. I would never get all these details, I would never know how or when to apply them, and I would never have the power that should be behind each strike. Besides, it had only been two weeks since I found out I was the damned Heart Maiden, the only one who could bring salvation to the tziganes, whatever that meant. Since the ritual, when we found out my real powers, I had been treated like royalty. Whenever I came to the enclave, tziganes stopped and stared and smiled and bowed their heads with their fists over their hearts. Some dared come to me and ask for a blessing. A blessing! Me? Blessing someone? These people were doomed.

"Mirella," Artan called me, his voice much gentler than before, but like anything coming out of Artan's mouth, it still had an edge to it. "Let's start over."

Why did I feel so attracted to him? There was a very frustrating and unbendable no-dating rule that came with being the heart maiden. No matter what, I wasn't to be touched. I was to live my life alone, serving the tziganes until my very last breath. Artan, with his huge sense of honor, would never even look at me with any interest.

I had to do the same.

Easier said than done.

I set my water down and turned around. Frustrated with my progress, or lack of—among other things—I folded my arms over my chest, leaned against the cubies, and faced him, my chin lifted. "Can't I just find the flowers and you and the other warriors do the fighting?"

His shoulders relaxed and his eyes fixed on mine. Artan

took two steps closer. The intensity of his gaze was too much for me, so I averted my eyes, pretending the weight lifting equipment and the treadmills and ellipticals on the other side of the training room were interesting.

Artan let out a long exhale. "We have to hope for the best scenario and the best scenario is that when you feel the call of the flower, we will go there, retrieve it, and come back. Simple as that. No complications, no unexpected encounters. But we need to prepare for the worst."

I returned my eyes to him. "And that would be being attacked by alchemists."

He nodded. "Among other things."

"Like?"

He paused. "Like revenants and other creatures I hope you never meet."

The images of those revenants attacking us in the parking lot of my old apartment flashed through my mind. Those foul vampire-like creatures. I shuddered, hoping I didn't encounter one ever again.

"If you're trying to instill bravery in me, you're doing a poor job," I said. "In fact, you're doing the exact opposite. I might not go after any flower if there are alchemists and revenants and other creatures waiting to attack us."

"To attack you," he corrected me.

I gaped. "You're making it even worse."

"But it's the truth." He moved another foot forward, and the light overhead hit just right, making the gold flecks in his hazel eyes shine like the sun. His gaze never faltered as he continued, "I'm not trying to scare you. I'm trying to prepare you. You have your magic, and with training, you'll probably be able to defeat them all easily and picking the flowers won't seem like a torture session. But alchemists are tricky. They come up with new potions every day. What if they create a potion to render our magic useless? What if my warriors and I are busy fighting more alchemists? You need to be able to defend yourself."

"Even if I could do it. Even if something clicked, and I suddenly learned all the moves you've been trying to teach me, and I could fight. I don't ..." I paused, because I wasn't sure admitting this made me a good person or exposed a weakness. "I don't think I'll ever be able to kill someone, no matter how bad they are."

Artan dipped his chin once. "I know. I get it. But perhaps you'll never need to. Again, we hope for the best scenario, even in a bad one. If we are attacked, and we have to fight, and you can't use your magic, then you have to protect yourself until I can get to you and protect you." He paused. "You know I'll do what I can to keep you safe."

I nodded while telling my brain not to transform his words into more. He was a warrior ordered to protect the heart maiden. It was his job. Nothing else.

Another wave of frustration rushed through me. Fighting, magic ... Even with magic, I was having problems.

To Darcy's dismay, I continued training with Sheila at the Bellville enclave, but it wasn't as easy as it was before. Now I had more magic, magic I didn't know before, but it was also unstable. Sheila thought that if I had access to tiny amounts of magic at a time, I would learn how to control it, and then I could add on more.

"Think of it like your ballet classes," she had said. "You start in the beginner class. When you learn all there is to learn at that level, you move on to the intermediate class. You might feel overwhelmed right away, but with practice, you'll learn all the new moves at the new level of difficulty. And, later on, you move on to advanced classes. Same thing with your magic. If we access a tiny drop first and you learn to control that, we can add a little more. Then a little more. Then a little more."

It made sense. I agreed to it right away, and to do that, we used my mother's suppressing elixir. My mother adjusted the dosage accordingly, and she always gave me a little less right after I was supposed to have a lesson with Sheila. Of course, the elder council from the Lovell enclave didn't want me taking the elixir.

"They will punish you," my mother had said in a warning tone, but I knew her. Even if we had spent months apart, I still knew her. The way she said it, the tightness in her voice and the way she avoided my gaze, there was more to it. Perhaps punishing was a good word compared to whatever was on her mind.

Forcing my mind back to the present, I said to Artan, "I know."

"Good." Artan returned to the center of the mat. "Let's get going, then." He adjusted his stance—feet apart and most of his weight on his back leg in what he called a fighting stance, and fists raised.

During my first fighting class, Artan overloaded my brain with new terms. He had said that fighting styles changed, but the moves and strikes were always the same, even if their names changed from jiu-jitsu to kung fu, for example. Regardless, it was too much for my brain. Front stance, fighting stance, horse stance, inside-outside block, spear hand, two hand center chop, two fist middle block, knife hand chop, hammer kick, snap kick, jumping snap kick, side kick, turning side kick, roundhouse kick, back kick, hook kick, back wheel kick ... it was endless, and for someone who had never thought about fighting before, it was all Greek.

Besides, as I had told him, he was trying to teach me years of practice and learning in a few weeks. I was good with memory and choreography and new steps, but dancing and fighting were different.

Suppressing a groan, I met him in the middle of the mat and mirrored his stance.

"Feet wider," he said. I adjusted my stance. "Hands tighter." I tightened my fists. "Shoulders relaxed. But don't slump them."

Holy shit …

"Just get on with it!" I snapped.

Artan's jaw ticked. "Small steps." His tone was firmer than before. "First, you need to know how to—"

Tired of this shit, I attacked. Artan hadn't expected it, and I landed my snap kick right in his stomach, drawing out his breath. But Artan recovered quickly and blocked my second kick. Next, he blocked my punch and my roundhouse kick.

Then, he attacked.

I twisted my arms, trying to remember which block or parry I should use with each attack. My frustration grew, and when I finally decided on one, I used the wrong kind of block. Artan kicked my arms, sending my hands into an arc around me and making me lose balance.

I splat on the floor with a loud humph.

Again.

His eyebrows curled down, Artan knelt beside me. Leaning his torso over my fallen figure, he extended his hand to me.

I locked my eyes on his, once more amazed by the golden streaks in his eyes. He had to know his effect on me. No? Was he blind? Or clueless? Did he do it on purpose, or was he interested in me?

Before I could formulate any sort of answer or action, heavy footfalls filtered from the hallway into the training room and a new voice boomed, "What is going on here?"

3

THERON STARED FROM ARTAN TO ME AND BACK TO ARTAN, HIS dark eyes narrowed.

As swift as a cat, Artan jumped three feet back. "We were training," he said.

I frowned. What happened to the hand offering to help me up? What happened to staring into my soul?

Cursing under my breath, I pushed to my feet.

"Right," Theron drawled, walking to the mat. Theron was a warrior through and through. Tall, strong, with too many muscles and a chiseled face. His long dark hair, which was loose and down to his shoulders most of the time, gave him a dangerous flavor. "That was exactly what was happening." He turned to me. "I thought we had agreed I was sparring with you today."

I tilted my head at him. "No, it's tomorrow."

He tsked. "No, it's today."

"I have it on my calendar." I marched back to the cubies, where my phone was beside my water. "Here ... shit, today is Tuesday. I could swear it was Wednesday."

Theron arched an eyebrow, a smug grin on his lips. "See?" He faced Artan. "It's my turn to spar with her."

"That's not what the council ordered," Artan protested.

Theron advanced. "Do I look like I care about what your council says?"

Artan held his ground. "*Our* council. At least it's Mirella's and she's with us now."

Theron hissed, "She's with both enclaves."

Two tall, strong men facing each other with death shining in their eyes—it wouldn't end well.

"Guys," I called, but they didn't hear me.

"Her mother is Lovell, so—" Artan started.

Theron interrupted him. "Her mother was banished from—"

"—she's a Lovell too, which means—"

"—this enclave as if she had sided with—"

"—she has to do whatever the council—"

"—the alchemists and actually helped them—"

I rolled my eyes. It was like that almost every day. Artan and Theron arguing about which enclave I belonged with, and whom I would obey. One, I didn't belong to either enclave. I was still my own person, and even though I had accepted I was a tzigane, that was as far as I was willing to go. And two, I obeyed my wishes. I had stopped listening to my mother over a year ago. Why would I be ordered around by two greedy enclaves?

I had already agreed to train in magic and fighting with both enclaves—with some restrictions. They had already consumed all my free time. I barely had time to study or dance. I sighed.

And the guys continued arguing.

Damn it. Until a couple of minutes ago, I had thought

today was Wednesday, when in fact it was Tuesday. I glanced at the time on my cell phone. Almost three in the afternoon. If I left right now, I could still make it to my first dance class of the evening.

I opened my mouth to tell them I had to go, but then shut it again. I didn't need to tell anyone what I was doing, not even Artan and Theron. I was tired of their babysitting, and since they were so engrossed in each other, I knew I had found a great time to sneak out.

I grabbed my water and my tote, and walked out of the room as if I had stolen their swords and was about to run away with them.

Thankfully, neither of the guys noticed—great babysitters those two. They kept arguing like an old married couple.

Nowadays, I felt like I was only myself in the dance studio. Probably because no one followed me inside the studio classroom. I could close the door and leave the tziganes, the heart maiden, and even Theron and Artan behind.

There was nothing else but my students and me and the dancing.

Now, if only I could come back here after my college classes tonight and dance by myself for at least an hour, then I would feel better. Then, I would feel like I would be able to face the next day.

As I took a shower after my two dance classes, I formulated a plan. I was going to go to my chemistry class now, then instead of going to my mother's house and to bed early, I was going to come back here and dance. Hopefully, I would still be in bed by midnight. I shuddered, thinking I had an early start tomorrow morning. I had magic practice with Sheila at Bellville before my late morning ballet class—and Bellville was about forty minutes from town.

I sighed as I got dressed—my favorite ripped jeans, a beige blouse with some lace on the neckline, my brown leather boots, and a thin brown suede jacket with fringes on the back. Gold and silver bracelets on my arms and big golden hoops on my ears, and I felt more like myself. My previous self. The one I fought to be since I became the heart maiden. Damn, since I found out I was a tzigane.

Before becoming the heart maiden, I usually took the bus from the dance studio to the university. After, my mother or Artan or Theron would drive me. But since I had been able to fool them all—mom had dropped me at the studio after I told her I would be there all night—I decided to walk. It wasn't too far, and I had a few minutes to spare. I could use the peace and quiet. I took a deep breath, relishing the chilly October air. Soon, it would be too cold in Connecticut, and I didn't enjoy walking on slippery ice or snow-covered side-walks—another reason to enjoy a nice stroll right now.

With each step I took, I focused on clearing my mind.

I didn't want to think about anything. I didn't want to think about my life before. About how Phillip and his betrayal still hurt me. About how Sheila wanted to push my power. About how Darcy was an old hag who wanted to put a leash around my neck. How my mother and I were still walking on eggshells around each other. How Theron and Artan were always around me, mothering me and telling me what to do. How Ellie was trying hard to accept magic and supernatural creatures and other crazy concepts for my sake. How Annie's mother was relieved Annie wasn't the real heart maiden. How I was the heart maiden and the other tziganes treated me like a queen. Actually, like a delicate porcelain doll that could break at any second.

All tziganes but Theron and Artan, who loved to kick my ass when we were sparring.

I sighed and looked around the street. It was odd that neither of them were here by now. Usually, whenever I could sneak away from them, which was rare, they were on me in less than half an hour.

Enjoying my surprisingly extended freedom, I lifted my chin and inhaled deeply. The chilly air cooled my insides, making me calmer. Less worried. Less troubled.

It was almost seven in the evening, and the sky was already darkening. Even though I felt relatively safe walking from the studio to the university, soon it would be too dark to walk freely like that. Not that I thought anything would happen, but ... after being drilled about my safety so much over the past couple of weeks, it was starting to sink in.

But not enough that I didn't enjoy alone walks around town. For now.

As I approached the main entrance to the university campus, I noticed a long line of cars coming around the block. There was always a lot of movement around here, cars coming and going, but not stopped like this.

Then, I made the last turn down the road and saw it. The main entrance was closed and road workers filled the place. I walked closer, but even the sidewalk was closed.

"What happened?" I asked a worker who was waving his big hands, redirecting the traffic to the left so the cars could loop around and find one of the university side entrances.

"A pipe burst."

I frowned. "And you need to close the entire road and sidewalk for that?"

"Until we can locate where the pipe burst, yes."

Damn.

Groaning, I started following the cars to the left, so I too could use one of the side entrances. I glanced at the time on my cell phone and cursed under my breath. It would add another ten minutes to my walk with this detour. I would have to hurry or I would be late.

I halted in my tracks as something popped in my mind.

I glanced back, to the right of the closed entrance road. There was a public park there, and if I wasn't mistaken, walking trails, and one of them made a turn right behind the science building. Knowing I wouldn't make it in time if I stayed out here, I turned around and rushed toward the park.

The idea seemed pretty awesome, until I stopped at the start of the trail and glanced ahead. With the thick trees and the setting sun, the place was dark. Completely dark.

Shit.

I turned on the light on my phone, sucked in a sharp breath, and resumed walking.

It was eerily quiet on the trail, save for my steps on the dirt path. When I accidentally snapped twigs under my feet, I jumped out of my skin.

A couple of minutes down the trail, I was sure this wasn't my best idea.

All of a sudden, a squirrel ran across the path and I screamed. My hand over my heart, I cursed some more and tried to slow my breathing. Damn squirrel.

Scared out of my mind, I hurried my steps, chanting, *I'm stupid,* in my head.

A heavy cloud brushed against me, robbing me of my

breath. I froze in place as fear crawled into my veins, making it hard to move.

No, no, no, it couldn't be.

Focusing, I closed my eyes and sent my senses out. It rushed around me and bounced back from a thick wall of darkness to my right.

I snapped my eyes open, wide in terror.

The wall advanced, rolling in waves, taking everything, silencing it all.

Shit.

I jerked out of my shock and made it to a sprint.

And the alchemists appeared out of nothing, right in front of me. I turned around, ready to run back, but found myself surrounded. No less than six alchemists formed a wide circle around me.

I was dead.

"Come with us," one of them said.

Putting on a brave mien, I faced them all. It was hard, though, not to let their black clothes and the masks over the lower half of their faces scare me while processing how I would get out of this one. The odds didn't seem in my favor.

"In your dreams," I responded, sounding way braver than I felt.

"If you're going to be difficult ..." As if in a choreographed dance, the alchemists extended their hands, and their shadow swords appeared, shining against the dark clothes and the dark sky.

I gasped at their weapons and squeezed my phone tighter. Besides being the only light source, it was my only help. If only I could send a quick text to Theron, or start a call so he could hear me.

Or ... I could try reaching him through our mind connection.

He wouldn't get here in time, but he would know something happened. He would come after me, and he would save me. Again.

A shudder rolled down my spine.

When would I stop being the damsel in distress? When wouldn't I have to worry about walking down the street and being attacked?

Tired of being saved by Theron and Artan, I turned my focus within. Using the methods Sheila had taught me, I channeled my power. It flickered to life inside me, weak from the elixir I had drunk earlier, but alive.

I pulled on it, trying to dig it out from wherever it was buried, trying to make it grow ten times, fifty times, despite everything. Exhaustion washed over my bones and muscles as if I were trying to lift a huge weight from the floor—and failing.

"One last chance to surrender," the alchemist said.

And what? Let them kill me and harvest my blood? I would rather die fighting.

Shit ... fighting. If only I had learned something while sparring with Artan or Theron. If the alchemists turned on me with those swords, all I could do was run. Where? There was nowhere to go.

All I could do was use my magic—my limited magic.

"Come and get me," I barked.

The alchemist grunted as he charged me.

I stepped back, lifting an invisible wall right where I had been. The alchemist bumped into it and stumbled back.

"What the—?"

I smiled, proud of myself.

Until two pairs of hands closed around my upper arms. Panic rose in my chest and I lost a grip on my magic.

"That was pathetic," the brute holding my left arm said.

The one grasping my right arm looked out to the other alchemists getting closer. "Are you sure she's the heart maiden?"

"Positive," one of them answered. He dipped his chin once. "Let's get out of here."

The brutes started dragging me back.

The panic rose to my throat, choking me.

I was so dead.

No, not yet.

Focus, Mirella.

Sheila had told me time and time again that I had to focus. There would be times, she said, that I would have to use my magic while all I wanted to do was curl into a ball and scream or cry. And still I had to push through and use it.

I closed my eyes and concentrated. Like I had done once before, I sent my senses out and found the minds of the brutes dragging me away. A thick wall surrounded their minds, but I wasn't fazed. I probed and searched and poked until I found a tiny small crack. I pushed in with all I had.

I got in.

Screaming, the two brutes let go of me—I fell on my butt —and knelt on the ground, their hands over their heads as horrifying pain exploded within every millimeter of their brains.

Two others lunged at me, but pushing through my own pain and tiredness, I had them on their knees before they could touch me.

The magic was taking its toll, and I blinked as exhaustion made it hard to focus. But I had to ... I had to ...

The remaining two alchemists came at me. I tried reaching for their minds, but I had no energy left to prod and poke around until I found an opening.

"Stop!" one of the alchemists shouted. A moment later, his foot was on my chest, pushing me down. Without any strength left, I lay on the ground as he stepped on my chest and pointed his shadow sword at my neck. "Let them go."

Without a choice, I released my magic on the other alchemists. They stopped screaming and shook their hurting heads, trying to recover from the miserable pain. I felt instant relief, but not enough to fight back.

Even if I knew some cool moves like Artan and Theron, now I didn't have the strength to use them.

The alchemist pressed the tip of the sword into my skin. I gasped, as if I could move farther away from it. "Don't try anything funny again. I have to take you in alive, but that doesn't mean I can't hurt you."

Shit.

Desperation bloomed in me and tears burned the back of my eyes.

There was nothing more I could do. I had even lost my phone somewhere on the dirt path. All I could do was hope they wouldn't kill me as I tried reaching Theron's mind. Someone had to know what happened to me, even if he didn't find me in time.

I sent my senses out, but I was weak and it was hard to maintain it, to search for Theron. I looked for him at the Lovell enclave—the last place I had seen him—but he wasn't there. I sent my mind to Bellville ...

My head whipped to the side and pain exploded in my cheek, spreading through my face. I was so exhausted, I could barely scream in pain and anger.

"Stop whatever you're doing," the alchemist said, his hand still extended from the slap he gave me. The other alchemists grabbed my arm and pulled me up.

I stumbled to my feet. The alchemist pressed my back to his chest, his hands tight on my arms. I jerked against him.

The other alchemists closed his fist and showed it to my face. "I will—"

"Take your hands off her!"

4

———

HIS SWORD RAISED AND READY FOR A FIGHT, THERON STEPPED onto the dirt path directly into the weak light coming off my phone a few feet in front of me.

"I said get your hands off her," he repeated, his tone stinging with a bite. There was murder in his eyes as he stared down the alchemists.

Two alchemists pulled me back, while the other four formed a line in front of me, their shadow swords in hand.

"It looks like we get another tzigane for free," one of the alchemists said.

Theron's lip curled up in one of his trademark cocky smirks. "Dream on."

And then he attacked.

I only saw Theron's sword coming down before someone stepped on my phone and the light went out. Darkness surrounded us. My heart trembled as the clank of the metal and the grunts and heavy footfalls on the dirt path were the only things I heard, and those didn't let me know who was winning.

I screamed as the alchemists dragged me farther away from Theron. My head hurt and my brain was fuzzy, but I still jerked against them, trying to get free.

Two quick humphs sounded right by my ears, and I was dropped on the ground, falling hard on my butt.

Again.

A flashlight shone in my face.

"Are you okay?"

I gasped, recognizing that voice. "Mom?"

She turned the flashlight up and then I could see her face. "Yes, I'm here." She leaned over me, her eyes searching my face. "Are you okay? Did they hurt you?"

"I'm ... I'm gonna be fine. I think." Pushing through the dizziness, I reached for the flashlight. "Theron. We need to help Theron."

My mother pointed the flashlight toward the grunts and gasps, and Theron buried his sword in the alchemist's stomach to the hilt. Teeth gritted, he pulled the sword out and the alchemist's body fell on the ground with a thud.

The alchemists were all on the ground. All six of them.

Theron turned to me and his expression softened. "Hey, are you okay?" He jogged to me and put his blood-covered sword into the scabbard before reaching down, grabbing my hand, and helping me up.

"I'm—" I swallowed the word fine as I swayed on my feet.

Theron hooked his hands under my elbows to keep me steady. "You're not fine." His grip on me tightened. "What the hell were you thinking? Sneaking off like that?"

I scoffed. "As if I could. You guys have my schedule down to the minute. I bet that if you really wanted, you could even guess which store I was walking by at a certain time."

Theron groaned. "It doesn't matter. You sneaked off. You can't do that."

I pushed against him, trying to make him let go, but he didn't budge. "Why not? I'm free to do whatever the hell I want."

"Not anymore, no," he barked. "You're the heart maiden, by Saint Sara-la-Kali. Our entire community depends on you."

I inhaled a sharp breath. "That's a lot to put on a single person."

"I know," he said in a sigh. "I know, but we can't change that. It is what it is, and you need to accept it."

Using one of the moves I did remember from my lessons with Artan, I moved my elbows up then out, finally making Theron lose his grip on me.

Still dizzy, I tripped back and would have fallen, again, if my mother hadn't stepped in, winding her arm around my waist.

"She needs a healer," she said to Theron.

"No, I just need to rest," I protested.

"It doesn't matter," my mother said. "We need to go back to Lovell, and there a healer will see you."

I groaned. "I'm not going back to Lovell today." Shit ... my plans of going to class, of dancing later tonight ... it went all down the drain. How would I dance if I was so dizzy I could barely stand on my own? Still, I wasn't going to Lovell. "I want to go home and rest."

My mother shook her head. "No, sweetie. The council called an urgent meeting. We're going to Lovell."

"Urgent meeting." I lifted my chin to Theron. "Were you invited to this urgent meeting?"

Theron pressed his lips tight. "No. No one in Bellville was."

"Then, it's not urgent," I protested. "We agreed that when it was urgent, when it affected all tziganes, Lovell would call on Bellville too."

The animosity between the enclaves was still thick and raw, even after I made the leaders agree that they would work together. I understood it was hard to erase two hundred years of animosity in only a couple of weeks—after all, both enclaves felt betrayed and misunderstood.

Two hundred years ago, there was only Lovell. Damara was the name of the heart maiden back then. She was the only one able to sense when the heart flower bloomed and where it was. She was the only one who could follow its call and touch the flower. After finding the heart flower, she extracted the liquid from inside it—and that liquid, the heart elixir, was sacred. It was magical and tziganes depended on it for their magic and for their health.

However, as the heart maiden, Damara wasn't to be touched. Not lovingly, not by a man who loved and desired her. Regardless, Damara couldn't control her heart. She fell in love with Emilian, and he fell in love with her. When the elder council found out, they had Emilian executed.

Feeling betrayed by the turn of events, Emilian's family up and left the enclave, creating their own, with looser rules and more understanding. However, after Emilian's death, Damara lost it and killed herself too. And for two hundred years, there hadn't been a new heart maiden ... until me.

Theron scooped me up in his arms. "Regardless, we need to get you out of here."

I protested as Theron carried me down the trail with my

mother following close on his heels, but they ignored me as usual.

Light shone from the end of the trail, and as we stepped out into the main area, lampposts illuminated the park and beyond the parking lot, where Theron's Jeep and my mother's car were parked side by side.

I frowned. "How did you know where to find me?"

Theron glanced at me, his dark eyes hard. "We didn't. I mean, we knew you had chemistry class this evening. Artan went to the science building, but he said you never arrived. Sloan checked the dance studio and you had already left. Cora drove by all the possible routes from the studio to the university and didn't see you."

My stomach sank. "You guys were out looking for me."

He stared straight ahead, but I could see from the tension in his neck and jaw that he was mad at me. "Yes. We had several warriors out searching for you in several possible places." Then, his eyes softened a little and he glanced at me again. "You gave us quite the scare."

"I'm sorry," I muttered.

My mother slipped behind the wheel of her car, and Theron deposited me in the passenger seat beside her. "The important thing is that you're safe now."

My mother looked at Theron. "*Nais tuke.*"

I frowned. "Nae what?"

"*Nais tuke,*" my mother repeated in a low voice. "It means thank you, dear."

Another word in tzigane I didn't know ...

Theron retreated from the car and answered my mother, "No problem. See you later."

"Wait, aren't you coming?" I asked him. "I want you at this urgent meeting."

"I'm gonna wait for the others," he said, his voice tight. I could see that not being invited to the meeting bothered him too. "They are coming to help me clean this mess up."

"Oh."

He closed the car's door and waved as my mother peeled away from the parking lot.

———

My mother didn't say anything as she drove out the park and out of town, but I could see in the way she gripped the wheel tight, and the way her lips were pressed into a thin line, that she was holding out on a long sermon.

Finally, in the quiet and darkness of the interstate, she cracked. "Here." She offered me a small vial.

I took the vial and lifted it before my face. In the dark, I could only make out a clear liquid inside. "What's this?"

"A mild healing elixir. It'll help you with the dizziness and the pain."

I brought it to my lips, but the acrid smell coming from the vial reached my nose, and I almost gagged. "What is in this thing?"

"You might not want to know. Just drink it."

Clamping my nose, I downed the liquid. It burned my throat and the aftertaste was even worse than the smell. I placed a hand over my mouth, forcing myself to keep the contents of my stomach inside.

"That was horrible," I muttered. Like magic, it didn't take ten seconds for the elixir to work. The pain in my face and body lessened and the dizziness and weakness retreated. I still needed a good night's sleep, but at least now I was sure I wouldn't faint while talking to the council.

I groaned on the inside. Damn, the council.

I glanced at my mother, at her tension rolling in waves over me. She was driving us to Lovell. Nothing I said would change her mind about it.

I sighed and opened my mouth to ask her more details about the meeting.

She surprised by letting out a grunt, then barking, "By Saint Sara-la-Kali, why do you do this? Why do you run away from the people trying to protect you? Why are you so careless with your own life?"

"I—" I started, though I wasn't sure what I would say.

My mother kept going. "I thought … I thought you understood what's going on here. What you are, what you mean to our enclave. To all tziganes."

My relationship with my mother had never been easy. When I was little, I thought she was crazy. Talking to plants and palm reading? Who did that? Only a crazy person.

Now I knew better. But that didn't change the fact that she lied to me my entire life. That she had concealed my powers for years.

I groaned. "I don't want to be this heart maiden thing."

My mother gasped and she looked at me as if I had slapped her. "Don't say that," she said, her tone low. Disappointed. She returned her attention to the road. "Never say that. Being the heart maiden … that's an incredible honor."

"How can you say that? Just a few weeks ago, you were still trying to hide my magic."

"Because I didn't know what would happen to you!" she yelled. She took a long breath and continued in her normal tone. "You were out there, alone, without an enclave. You didn't want to accept Lovell as your enclave and—"

"I still don't."

"I didn't know the extent of your powers. I mean, I always knew you were powerful. I just didn't know you were *this* powerful."

I glanced at my hands folded on my lap. There was supposed to be immense power inside these hands. Well, I had felt it all once, during the ceremony—and it had been so powerful, it overtook me and I fainted from its intensity. Since then, I kept it in check with one of the many elixirs my mother made for me. Since then, I hadn't felt the strength of my magic, not in its entirety. Since then, I didn't want to.

"I didn't ask to be this powerful."

My mother reached over and her hand rested on top of mine. "I know, dear, I know. But you are. You're the beloved and blessed heart maiden. You can do wonderful things for the tzigane community. All you have to do is accept it."

I inhaled deeply. "And with that accept that my life isn't my own anymore."

"You know, some say that the secret to happiness is making others happy. When you help others, you're helping your own soul. That's what a heart maiden does."

There was truth in her statement, but that didn't make it any easier to give up everything I wanted and was. I wanted to live on my own, not in an enclave. I wanted to go to college and dance classes, not attend magic and fighting lessons. I wanted to go out with Ellie like a normal girl without my bodyguards following my every step.

I just wanted to be normal.

Thankfully, my mother didn't push the topic anymore the rest of the drive to Lovell.

Once we approached the enclave, the warriors opened the gates and let us in without any explanation. My mother parked the car behind the main house, and we were escorted by two warriors through the streets of Lovell.

There were lampposts and lights spread throughout the narrow streets, illuminating the terracotta-colored houses and buildings, tinting them with an even warmer glow. At this time of the night, most people were inside their houses, having dinner, getting ready for bed … we walked past only a couple of tziganes, who stopped and acknowledged me as if I was the queen out for a stroll. When they were out of sight, I shook my head, certain I would never get used to it.

The warriors escorted us across the main square, into the main two-story building, and to the council room, where two other warriors stood. Upon seeing me, they opened the doors and let us pass.

I was still tired and a little dizzy and frustrated with everything that had happened, but I lifted my chin and walked right in. My mother, on the other hand, hunched her shoulders and stood by the doors, as if afraid she would break some rule and be banished again.

As I approached the curved table, Darcy, seated at the center, smiled at me—her full-teeth, old hag creepy grin.

"Mirella," she said, her tone sharp. "I heard you had an encounter with alchemists a few moments ago. Are you okay now?"

"Yes, I'm okay."

"My dear. That wouldn't have happened if you stopped neglecting your duties."

Frustration surged inside me. "I've been training in magic and fighting, just as you asked. You've already taken up my free time. What else do you want?"

Her smile slipped away. "I want you to start acting like the heart maiden."

I stood tall, fighting the urge to put my hands on my waist and roll my eyes at her. "And how is a heart maiden supposed to act?"

"A heart maiden dedicates her entire heart and soul to the tziganes. Her sole duty is to learn how to control her magic and find the heart flower."

I gritted my teeth. Since the awakening ceremony, tziganes kept asking me if I was hearing the call from the heart flower. When was I going after the flower? When I was going to bring it back to the enclave so they could use it?

But so far, I hadn't heard any call. I hadn't felt any tug. Nothing.

"I'm doing the best I can," I said, my voice tight.

"Perhaps your definition of doing your best isn't the same as ours."

My frustration spiked. I buried my hands on my hips. "What is that supposed to mean?"

"As heart maiden, you should quit college and dancing," she said, resolute. I would be shocked if we hadn't had this same argument at least three times in the last two weeks. Maybe I wouldn't feel so caged and robbed if the council actually heard me and worked with me. "It's your duty."

Dozens of retorts jumped to my tongue, but I bit them back. I was impressed with my control. If it had been a month ago, I would have spat curses at her.

However, that didn't mean I was going to stand here and let them boss me around.

I tsked. "Then maybe I don't want to be your heart maiden anymore."

With that, I turned around and marched toward the exit.

"Young lady, wait," a new voice called. Taking a long breath, I halted. I knew that voice. It was Oscar, Darcy's son and Artan's father. Slowly, I turned around. Beside his mother, Oscar stood from his chair. "The tziganes need the heart flower, Mirella. If we can't find a flower and make an elixir and spread its power to all of us, we will fall sick. Very sick."

I knew that, but I thought we still had time. "You had a spare flower for the ceremony a few weeks ago. Don't you have any flowers left?"

"That was the last one," Oscar said. "We need more flowers, Mirella, because people have been falling ill."

I gasped. A heavy ball settled in my stomach. "Since when?"

"The first signs started two days ago," he said. "At first, we thought it could be a cold, but we can confirm it now. It's the heart sickness."

Darcy stood. "Which means, we need the flower as soon as possible, or more and more tziganes will fall sick."

"And become sicker," Oscar added.

Dika, an old woman with light brown hair and warm hazel eyes, stood from her chair behind the table. "Please, Mirella. My daughter is one of the sick people. You need to focus and find the flower."

My throat went dry. "I-I'll work harder," I said, my voice low. Not sure how I would work harder than I already was. Maybe if I gave up sleep? But I had to try.

Darcy sighed. "You're dismissed."

Feeling like I needed fresh air at once, I rushed out of the building, my mother following close behind.

"*Chey*, are you okay?"

I stopped right in front of the fountain and turned to her, rage spilling from my voice. "I'm tired of that damn question! Do you know how many times I hear that every day?"

She flinched. "Mirella, I'm just—"

"I'm going for a walk," I snapped.

I turned and started walking away.

I heard her soft voice as she said, "I'll wait by the house …"

Gritting my teeth, I hurried my steps.

The house. The damn house the council had set up for my mother and me *when* we decided to move to Lovell. Because to them it was a question of when, not if.

Though I had walked by the house before, I had never entered it, but I knew it was one of the best houses in the enclave.

I marched to the other side of the square and down one of the narrow streets between the long rows of houses, past the training grounds, until I was at the edge of the forest. I looked up, at the bright moon overhead, shining down upon me. I inhaled deeply, letting the crisp air fill my lungs and clear my mind.

Eyes closed, I heard the gurgle of water in the distance. During my first tour of the enclave, Ryane hadn't told me about the valley and the waterfall, but Artan had showed me after one of our first training sessions.

Now, in the semi-dark, I stared at the thick mess of trees, knowing they soon opened to a valley and, farther ahead, a lake with the alluring waterfall. The waterfall wasn't huge, but it looked inviting. I had promised myself to swim among the gray rocks once it was warmer and I had time.

Ha, time.

If I ever had any free time for myself again, I would be damn lucky.

"You shouldn't be out here alone." I stood my ground and didn't turn around as Artan approached me. He halted by my side, facing the trees. I was sure he would start a huge argument about how I shouldn't have run like that, and should be escorted by at least two warriors right now ... Instead, his next words surprised me. "What are we looking at?"

I didn't say anything for a minute. I stared at the trees and the leaves as they moved with the gentle breeze.

"Does any tzigane have the power to go back in time?"

Artan tilted his head at me. "Not that I know of."

"What a shame. I wish I could go back in time," I said. A daydream started in my mind. "If I could, I would like to go back to how things were before."

"Before becoming the heart maiden?"

I shook my head. "No, even before that. Right after I moved to Broken Hill, but before I met you and Theron and Phillip ..." I sighed. "Even before I met Ellie, if that meant I wouldn't have turned into the heart maiden. If that meant I wouldn't disappoint everyone."

Artan stepped right in front of me, his eyes narrowed. "One, it's not like you turned into the heart maiden. You were born the heart maiden. We just found out late. And two, you're not disappointing anyone."

I scoffed. "Have you talked to your grandmother lately?"

"Forget about her. She can be difficult at times, but we all know you're still getting used to the idea of being the heart maiden." He paused. "I'm not disappointed in you, and I'm sure you'll succeed." His words. Why did he have to say things that made my insides warm? "Especially if you work harder."

And then he threw a bucket of cold water over my head.

Grunting, I took a step back. "How am I supposed to work harder? Maybe if I don't sleep anymore. And then what? I faint from exhaustion each time we train?"

He reached for my hand. His fingers grazed over my skin, sending a jolt of goose bumps up my arms, but I took a step back.

"Mirella ..."

"Don't Mirella me," I snapped.

"I'm just trying to help."

For some reason, that only made me more irritated. More furious. "Well, then don't."

I stalked away.

I heard Artan calling my name a couple of times, but I ignored him.

From the start of our drive back to Broken Hill, the air inside the SUV was thick, and grew tenser by the minute. Behind the wheel, Artan's attention was fixed on the road. Theron lounged in the backseat. Despite looking relaxed, the tick of his jaw, the strain of his neck, and the narrowed eyes showed me how tense and angry he was.

We all were.

After walking away from Artan the night before, I ended up going to the house the elder council had given to my mother and me. I barged in, ready to demand my mother take us back to Broken Hill, but I found her asleep on the couch, a book on her lap, and tea on the side table beside her. My heart tugged. She looked so serene and small. For some reason, I didn't want to wake her up, so I grabbed the throw blanket from one of the armchairs and covered her. Thankfully, the couch looked comfortable and she wouldn't wake up with any neck or back pain in the morning.

Finding myself alone, I went exploring. The house was bigger on the inside than it looked from the outside, but it was warm and colorful and elegant. A large living and dining room to the left, a study-slash-library to the right, a foyer with wide wooden stairs in the middle, and a fancy kitchen with dark wooden cabinets and beige marble counters, a breakfast nook for six, and a screened porch in the back. Upstairs, I found the laundry room and three suites complete with sitting rooms and walk-in closets. One of the suites had a flower theme with lavender and white decorations—I was assuming this one was mine. My suspicion was confirmed when I got to the closet and saw a few clothing items—ripped jeans, blouses with lace and fringes, a couple of hipster dresses, and even pajamas and undies and bras and socks—all in my size.

I hoped my mother had bought all these in the name of the enclave, otherwise this was plain creepy. Well, judging by the fact I liked everything in here, I could only assume I was right. My mother knew what I would like and what I wouldn't.

Not wanting to give in, but without any options at that moment, I took a quick shower in the luxurious bathroom, put on the new pajamas, and went to bed. I hated to admit it, but the queen size bed with the fluffy pillow and comforter was perfect. However, each time I closed my eyes, I saw the alchemists attacking me, tying me up, and taking me away. My night was filled with nightmares.

The next morning, I woke up early and asked a warrior stationed at the front of the house—as I knew at least one would be—to tell the council I wanted to meet with them before going back to Broken Hill for my college classes. While I gave the warrior time to go gather the council members, my mother made us breakfast with the food in the fridge and pantry. I wondered once more when the council, or whoever, stocked this house. I noticed from her sharp movements that she wanted to talk to me, or ask something. But as usual, she kept it all bottled in, even after I had prodded her.

The council members didn't seem too happy to be meeting me so early, but once I started talking, they seemed to relax.

"I've come to a decision," I said. "It's the middle of the semester. I have only two more months before winter break, so for now I'll keep teaching dance and going to my college classes, because I signed up for those and I want to *honor* my agreements." I knew how tziganes were big on the whole honor thing, so I planned on using that card. "But starting next year, I'll teach only one or two dance classes and drop down to part time for my college classes. That should free another four or five hours of my days, and I'll dedicate these hours to training in magic and fighting."

The elders turned toward each other and debated my proposal.

Then after almost ten minutes, Darcy steepled her fingers and spoke up. "It's not the best solution, but we accept your decision. With two conditions." I knew that was coming. "One, you have to train in magic with someone from Lovell too." Which meant her. "And two, wherever you go, Artan and Sloan will go with you."

I pressed my lips tight, trying to keep all the curses at the tip of my tongue inside. After I was able to swallow them all, I said, "I'm okay with your first condition." Not really, but I knew she wouldn't concede if I pushed, not anymore. "But the second one is unfair. When I became the heart maiden, I was clear that I would be working with both Lovell and

Bellville. So, if you want two warriors to follow me around, then it has to be one from each enclave."

"Fine," she said, her voice tight. "You can ask Theron from Bellville to replace Sloan."

And that was how the two of them were taking me to Broken Hill early in the morning on a Wednesday so I could get to my first class of the day.

"I need a new cell phone," I said, breaking the silence.

"Right," Theron said from the backseat. "Yours got smashed last night."

"Yup."

"We can stop somewhere and buy you a new one after your classes," Artan offered.

I glanced at him. "Thanks."

Before going to BHU, we had to go to my mother's house to pick up my books. Since I had no idea I would be spending the night at Lovell, I hadn't brought them last night.

By some miracle, Artan and Theron hadn't exchanged one word or argued during the entire forty-five-minute drive from the enclave to Broken Hill. Until Artan parked in the driveway of my mother's house.

"I'll go in with her," Theron said, opening the backdoor.

"No, I'll go," Artan said, jumping out of the SUV.

Shaking my head, I grabbed my keys from my purse and walked to the front door, while the two of them argued about who would accompany me inside the house, who would open the door, who would make sure I was okay, who would go inside the classroom with me later, and who would stay outside walking around the building and making sure we were all safe. They hadn't even noticed they were already following me inside the house.

I tuned them out while I went upstairs and swapped the

books in my tote. I made sure to leave my dance tote ready too, since I had more dance classes later in the day, then I went downstairs to the kitchen to grab some granola bars—I liked to have a couple in my tote in case I got hungry between classes. All the while, the guys kept arguing.

These two.

I grabbed a couple more bars from the pantry and showed them to Theron and Artan. "You guys want some?" They quieted down immediately. "Wow, don't tell me you two love these things?" I shook the bars in the air.

Artan waved his hand at me. "Shhh."

I opened my mouth in a retort, but then I felt it. A tug in my gut, a tingling in my mind, a heavy feeling just outside the house, but it was a different feeling from last night.

"It's not alchemists," I whispered. I took a step closer to the guys, who already had their hands behind their backs, where I knew daggers were secured under their jackets. Walking around college campus with swords hanging from their waists would be too much for the *gadjos*.

"No," Theron responded in a low voice. "Revenants."

I gasped. Those again? "What ... no. They ... they are here for me?"

Artan shot me a hard look. "Who else?"

I swallowed the fear that surged in my chest.

Theron grabbed my arm and pulled me behind his back. "Think we can make a run for it?"

Artan looked out the windows as if the revenants would be right there, on the porch, waiting to come in. "I'm not sure. Either way, we should get ready."

Facing the kitchen door, Theron pushed me back and retreated into the hallway. "I say we run. If we can't make it, then we fight."

Artan scoffed. "And fight revenants outside in broad daylight? I don't think so."

Theron glared at him. "Then do you have a big idea?"

"As a matter of fact—"

"Stop!" I shouted. "You two act like little kids arguing all the time. It's driving me insan—"

With a loud boom, the back door flew off its hinges and the windows burst as revenants crawled inside the kitchen.

I froze, my eyes wide, as I stared at the creatures advancing on us. I had only seen them once before, and it had been at night. Now, they looked even creepier and scarier.

The creatures with rotting gray skin and pointy ears snarled at us, showing their razor-sharp teeth and two long fangs. They lifted their long limbs, as if ready to snatch us with their jagged claws.

I pushed down the panic rising in my chest.

Artan clamped a hand around my wrist and yanked me back. Holding a dagger, he stepped forward as a revenant launched at us. Theron was next, pulling me behind him too. He exchanged a few punches with a revenant before drawing the dagger hidden under his pants, strapped to his shin.

A swarm came in, and the warriors fought, while I watched and tried to rein in my panic.

I was tired of standing back like a delicate princess, though.

I hadn't drunk the suppressing elixir since yesterday afternoon, so I focused and woke up my powers. They obeyed a little easier, a little faster than yesterday, and soon my veins felt heavy and full as if it were about to explode.

A revenant lunged at me and I extended my hand, like I had practiced with Sheila, and let it out. My magic rushed down my arm and a ball of fire appeared in my hand. I threw the fire at the revenant. The vampire let out a roar when the ball hit him in the chest and spread over his entire body in a matter of seconds. My jaw hanging open, I watched as it turned into a pile of dust at my feet.

Giddiness filled my chest alongside the magic. All right, now these revenants were toast.

I turned to where Artan and Theron fought the throng of revenants, ready to let it all out—

Something warm started deep inside my chest, a warmth that wasn't mine. I gasped as the warmth became a ball of energy too big for my chest, and I fell on my knees.

"Mirella!"

I heard my name, but I couldn't tell who had said it. My vision became hazy and a strong scent surrounded me. I inhaled deeply—flowers. It wasn't roses, or violets, or daisies … I knew a lot of flower scents and none of them were this scent, this warm, this enthralling.

My hand shot to my chest, right above the warmth now surrounding my heart, and I gasped.

It was the heart flower.

6

"Mirella."

Someone grabbed my shoulders and shook me. "Mirella!"

The haze faded from my sight, and I saw Artan kneel in front of me, his hands gripping my shoulders.

"I'm here," I said, my voice hoarse.

Theron leaned over Artan to look at me. "What happened? Are you okay?"

I blinked and looked around. The bodies of several revenants littered my mother's kitchen, and there was blood everywhere—the floor, the wall, the cabinets. Even on the ceiling.

Disgust rolled in my stomach, and for a moment, I thought I was going to be sick.

"We should get out of here." Artan grabbed my hand and stood, pulling me with him. "See? This is why you can't wander around alone. Hell, you weren't alone. That's it. You're moving to Lovell immediately."

"What? No!"

Theron shook his head. "I hate to say this, but I agree with

Artan on this one. It has just become too dangerous for you out here. I'm sorry, but you can't stay in Broken Hill anymore."

"And that means your dance and college classes too," Artan said. "You can't go to them anymore."

I widened my eyes at him. "You don't have a say in this. That's not the agreement I have with the Elder Council."

Artan grunted. "It'll be once I tell them what happened here."

"You guys are turning me into a slave," I protested.

"We're trying to help you," Theron said, his tone harsh, harsher than he ever spoke to me. "We prefer to see you bored and safe than out here and ..." He gestured to the mess behind him.

I averted my eyes before I spilled the contents of my stomach on the floor.

"Besides, you're not ready," Artan said. "You need to train more. Fighting *and* magic." I groaned. "You just froze here. What was that? You were on your knees, doing what?"

The warmth in my chest answered, spiking and making me gasp. It hadn't gone away, but now that I focused on it, it flared again. The scent of the flower tickled my nose. "The flower," I whispered, afraid of breaking the spell. "The heart flower." Artan's eyes widened. Theron inhaled a sharp breath. "I can feel it."

"What?" Artan's voice pitched high. "You do? By Saint Sara-la-Kali."

Theron turned to him. "We need to follow it. We should call and put a team together ASAP."

"Yes." Artan nodded in agreement. "We should get a good team out there." He turned to me. "Where is it?"

I closed my eyes and focused on the feeling, on the

warmth, on the fire building inside me. I sniffed the air. Maybe if I followed the scent, but two steps out and the scent died. A second later, it filled my nostrils again. I took a couple of steps toward it, then it died. In circles I went, trying to pinpoint where it was coming from.

"I ..." I closed my eyes tighter and called on the warmth. *Please, please, show me where to go. Guide me.* But there was nothing. Besides feeling the flower, I had no idea where to go. Shoulders sagging, I opened my eyes and faced the guys. "I don't know."

"What do you mean you don't know?" Theron asked.

Embarrassed, I shrugged. "I just ... I don't know. I can feel it. I know it's calling me. I can even smell it, but I can't pinpoint where it's coming from."

Artan groaned. "No, this can't be happening."

"But you're the heart maiden," Theron said.

"I know!" I shouted. "Do you think I like this? I'm trying, but I can't tell where it's coming from."

Artan let out an exasperated sigh. "This can only be because you haven't trained enough. If only you had dedicated yourself—"

"Oh, just shut up, Artan," I snapped. "If you're frustrated, put yourself in my shoes. How do you think I feel?"

I didn't think any of them realized I was as frustrated and lost as they were. Even more than they were. I was supposed to be the one, the solution, their revered queen and guide. And I couldn't do shit.

I was a gigantic failure.

"Hey, hm, maybe we should take a step back and think," Theron said, his tone calmer but firmer, as if he were the referee trying to avoid a fight.

Avoiding looking at the kitchen, I turned around and started for the front door. "What I need is to go see Sheila."

RELUCTANTLY, ARTAN DROPPED THERON AND ME AT THE Bellville enclave, promising to come pick me up in a few hours. Meanwhile, he would get some warriors to help clean up the house in Broken Hill, and start moving our stuff to the house in Lovell. And he also promised to stop by a store and get me a new phone.

When we arrived, the ranch was quiet. It was a peaceful place, and I liked coming here more than I liked visiting Lovell. A large three-story house sat in the middle of the ranch, half covered by ivy, half painted in warm colors. Large, round windows and glass doors led to balconies and wrap-around porches.

As we walked across the estate, we found Marie, Annie, Bryna, and most of the kids having tea at one of the outside tables. When she saw me, Annie jumped off her chair and came running to give me a hug.

I opened my arms and humphed out loud when she threw herself at me, pretending she was too much for me. She laughed.

"Hi, sweet bun," I said, holding her tight. "How are you?"

She smiled at me. "Good."

I was glad to hear that. After all she went through, I couldn't bear hearing she wasn't well. Annie had been kidnapped by alchemists years ago. Though everyone thought she had been killed, the alchemists decided to use her because of her unique powers. Annie could sense other tziganes, sense their magic, and use it when she was near enough to it.

The alchemists had used her to find me.

Thankfully, I had found her in the end. The other tziganes helped me free her from the alchemists, and bring her back to her mother.

"Have you been dancing?" She nodded. "Studying?" She nodded again. "Eating right?" She nodded once more.

I took her to her mother, who once more held my hands and thanked me for finding and helping her daughter. I already told her she didn't need to do that, but I didn't think she would stop anytime soon.

Next, Theron and I found Ramon, Dolan, and Neil, who were in the five-car detached garage working on a car.

"What's wrong?" Theron asked, pausing at the entrance.

Neil was the first to turn around. "Mirella!" the *rom baro* of Bellville exclaimed. Dolan nodded his head at me, and Ramon glanced at me and grunted. For some reason, Theron's father always kept his distance from me, and Ramon seemed to hate me. But so far, he seemed to hate everyone. Neil cleaned his hands on a rag and came to greet me. "How are you?"

I groaned, hating to lie. So I didn't. "I could be better."

He frowned. "What's the matter?"

"I'm not sure yet," I said. "I'm hoping Sheila will be able to help me, though."

"Oh, mother can help anyone," Neil said, smiling.

Theron halted beside his brother and father and looked at the open hood of the beat up truck. They talked about car parts and problems, things I didn't understand at all, then Theron came back to me. "I'll take Mi to *puri daj*, then I'll be back to help you."

"Whatever," Ramon said in a grunt.

I tried not to take his sour mood to heart, but it was hard. He seemed to hate the world, and I didn't understand why.

Next, we found Cora, Rye, and Nico on the back porch. They waved at us and we waved back. Every time I looked at them, my heart clenched. The three of them weren't originally from Bellville. They had come to Bellville three years ago, after their enclave was ambushed and invaded by alchemists. The three of them were the sole survivors.

We walked past the house, to the garden in the back, where Sheila was tending to her plants.

Theron halted before his grandmother. "*Sastimos, puri daj,*"

An easy smile fell over Sheila's lips. She lifted her hands and wiggled her fingers. Theron took her hand in his and helped her up. She turned her warm eyes to me. "Hello, dear." She embraced me and I embraced her back. She wasn't my grandmother, but for some reason, she made me feel at ease, comfortable, treasured. She pulled back and searched my face. "What's troubling you?"

"I can feel the heart flower," I said. There was no reason to tiptoe around the topic with Sheila.

She gasped and her hands pressed against her chest. "You do? That's wonderful!"

Beside us, Theron groaned.

"No, it's not wonderful," I said. "I don't know where it's coming from. I can't follow it."

"Oh." Her face fell. "That is troublesome." She slipped her hand into mine. "Come. We'll fix this."

She took me through a peach-colored stone trail that whirled in and out of the lawn, until we were standing in front of a grotto, where the tall statue of Saint Sara-la-Kali stood. Instinctively, I placed my hand over my heart, feeling the pendant pinned between the strap and the pad of my bra. The liquid inside was gone, but there was something comforting about wearing the pendant, even if its effect wasn't the same anymore. Perhaps it was because of the engraving of the saint on it, or perhaps it was because I had worn it for so many years, I was simply used to it.

Sheila sat on the grass and pulled me down with her. Theron stood a few feet behind, watching.

I crossed my legs and squared my shoulders, ready to meditate. "What should I do?"

"First, close your eyes and focus on your power as we've practiced many times before."

I did as I was told. I shut my eyes and tried calling on my power. Besides the warmth of the flower filling my chest and making it hard for me to channel my magic, there was another issue.

I sighed.

Theron was behind me in a moment, his hand on the hilt of his sword. "What is it?"

"It's ..." I opened my eyes and glanced at Sheila. "It's Felix. He's prodding at my mind, asking for me."

Sheila shook her head. "That lion. He hasn't been the same since he bonded with you."

"He won't stop unless I come to him, or ..." I turned my eyes to Theron. "Or he comes here."

Theron's jaw hit the floor. "You mean, let the lion loose? Have you seen the size of that animal?"

I almost rolled my eyes at him. Of course, I had seen the size of the lion. Despite everyone's protests, I had even spent some time with him inside his cage. "He won't do anything.

You know he won't. He's like a big pet now. Unless you attack him first."

"I don't think that's a good idea."

"Are you sure he'll behave?" Sheila asked.

I nodded once. "Yes. All he wants is to stay by my side while I'm here."

"You understand that, if he attacks, we'll have to defend ourselves," Sheila said. "We'll have to hurt him."

"I know. He won't attack, I promise."

Sheila inhaled a sharp breath. "Theron, open his cage."

"But, *puri daj*—" She simply turned her brown eyes to him, and he snapped his mouth shut. "Yes, *puri daj*."

Theron marched away and Sheila looked at me with a smile. "Tell me, dear, what else is bothering you?"

"Nothing," I said too quickly.

She tilted her head at me. "I know you, Mirella. I understand if you don't want to talk to me about it, but don't lie to me."

"I'm sorry." I sighed. "It's just ... I was attacked by alchemists last night—"

"I know."

"—and this morning by revenants."

Sheila's eyebrows slammed down. "That's new."

"Yes, it just happened. Artan is on his way back there right now to clean it all up and ... dispose of the bodies." My stomach turned.

"It's too dangerous for you out there."

"I know. And that's what's bothering me. I have no choice but to move to Lovell now." I perked up. "Unless, I could move here."

Sheila let out a hollow chuckle. "No, dear. As much as I care for you, as we all care for you, we're not ready to take on the full wrath of Lovell. We're finally starting to patch things up with them. I won't let anything compromise that. Besides, you have to know, you'll be safe there."

"I know," I whispered. "But that's just one more step in their plan to take over my life."

She reached over and took my hand in hers. "I'm so sorry, dear, but there's nothing we can do about that. I hope you can find a balance between being yourself and being the heart maiden."

"I hope so too, but honestly, I don't see that happening any time soon."

"I understand. Just know that, as the heart maiden, you're everything to us." She squeezed my hand. "Use that to your advantage. Lovell and the elder council might give you a hard time about it, but remember, without you, they are nothing." She winked.

A small smile tugged at my lips. She was right, as usual.

I felt him in my mind before I heard his big paws advancing through the garden. I twisted my torso and my smile widened when Felix emerged from behind the tall hedges.

Felix was a heart animal—a rare creature with powers similar to ours. His fur was white and iridescent, and he was huge, much larger than a normal lion.

Hi, I said in his mind.

Like a big dog, he plopped down beside me, his snout touching my leg.

Are you okay now?

Images of lush forests and colorful flowers and bright blue skies exploded in my mind, and I assumed that meant that everything was all right. Felix didn't communicate with words, but rather with images and feelings he projected in my head.

I ran my hand over the top of his head, still amazed by how soft his fur felt against my skin.

I need to train a little. Will you let me?

He nodded his big head once, and I chuckled.

Sheila stared at the lion with big, round eyes. "It still boggles my mind."

"Mine too," Theron said, appearing in the clearing. "As soon as I opened the cage, he dashed here as if the place was on fire." One corner of his lips tugged up. "I guess he loves you."

I leaned over Felix and placed a soft kiss on his forehead. "At least someone does." Sheila opened her mouth to probably protest my statement, but I hadn't mentioned it to get coddled, so I said before she could, "He'll behave so we can train now."

"Right." Sheila shifted her weight. "All right. Let's start over. Close your eyes and focus."

Like before, I followed Sheila's instructions and we began training.

7

I SPENT THE REST OF THE WEEK TRAINING—MAGIC AND A LITTLE bit of fighting. The elder council insisted I focused on magic since I had to find the heart flower, but Artan mentioned I needed more combat training too. When we went out for the flower, I would need it, he said. So the council allowed it.

After spending Wednesday with Sheila at Bellville—and having a great meal with all the Bellville tziganes—Artan picked me up and brought me to my new home. It was weird entering the house, knowing this was it. This was when I became a prisoner.

But I decided to not let that get me down. Instead, I focused on training. Since the elder council wanted to keep an eye on me, Sheila started coming over for our sessions, and I also had to take lessons from Darcy. She seemed too eager to teach me, to show me she was the best, better than Sheila. I couldn't deny she was powerful, but her power didn't help mine.

Besides, the only reason I was taking lessons was because they thought it would be easier for me to find out how and where to follow the heart flower if I had a better handle on my magic. It seemed reasonable, but after a week of fourteen-hour days training and no advancement, either on finding the flower or handling my magic, I was exhausted and even more frustrated.

And I hadn't been sleeping well.

Frustrated even with that, I got out of bed early Friday morning, and after freshening up, I went for a walk at the edge of the forest, where I always felt calmer. Lonelier. Even if I knew there were warriors following my every step.

I stopped by the edge of the forest, in the same spot Artan found me the other night while I looked out at the trees. Focusing, I closed my eyes and listened. The ruffle of the leaves by the breeze, the squirrels on the trees, the waterfall a ways down the valley.

I sent my senses out and felt everything, like one of the first lessons Sheila taught me, before I had known who I was. What I was. I felt the leaves falling from the trees, the ants and spiders and other bugs crawling on the forest floor. I felt the water rushing down the rocks and forming a deep lake at the end of the valley.

But I didn't feel the heart flower.

The warmth inside my chest never left, though. It lessened during certain times of the day, and it also increased, bringing in the scent of the flowers. And yet, I couldn't reach it. I couldn't grab it and follow it.

I snapped my eyes open and groaned. Why was it so difficult? What was I missing? What was I doing wrong? How was I going to find it? It was like searching for a needle in a haystack.

I let out a long breath, as if I could expel all the bad things from my life with a simple exhale, and started back to the narrow streets of the enclave. I had training with Darcy in about half an hour and I still needed to have breakfast. I wasn't really hungry, but I needed some energy if I was going to practice all day.

Not really in a rush to start with my duties, I took the long way home, strolling down the stone streets winding around the enclave, and taking in the colorful sight. I might have my issues with Lovell and the elder council, but the enclave was a beautiful, warm, and lively place. Though I wouldn't admit it, I kinda loved it here.

As if fate wanted to sour more of my mood before the day had barely began, Artan crossed my line of sight, marching down the next street. What gave me pause, though, was the fact that a handful of kids trailed him.

Curiosity took root deep inside me and before I processed my thoughts, my legs moved and I followed him along an uphill winding path.

Another handful of kids—mostly boys ranging from eight to twelve years old—stood at the entrance of the training building. Once Artan went in, the kids followed him. I tried stopping, but my curiosity was just too strong ...

Besides, if I were to be honest, I didn't want to stop. Right now, I really wanted to see what Artan was up to.

He walked right past the room where we usually practiced and went to the back, to a larger room—dark gray mats lined the floors and racks of weapons filled the walls.

"Get the swords," Artan said, pointing to a large wooden box to the side. The kids rushed forward and came back to the center of the room with wooden practice swords.

Most of them smiled while they twirled the swords in their hands, visibly eager to start practicing and learning how to wield such weapons. As for me, I could barely punch the right way ... I would never train with swords.

The smaller kid, a boy who had probably just turned eight, tried imitating the older kids and dropped his sword on the mat.

Artan turned his known glare to the kid. "Paddy, stop playing around."

Keeping his head low, the kid scooped up the sword from the floor then stood still, as if even breathing might bring Artan's wrath upon him.

I frowned.

So he wasn't just hard on me. He was hard on the kids, too.

Two kids rushed by me, clearly late to the practice session. The commotion made Artan turn, his brow furrowed again. "What the—" the words of reproach came to a halt when he saw me standing by the door. His eyes widened. "Mirella, what are you doing here?"

"Mirella?"

"The heart maiden?"

"Where?"

The sixteen kids stared at me with stunned faces, as if I was either a ghost who came to haunt them, or a queen who should have been locked away in her tower.

I sighed and waved at them. "Hi there." The kids bowed at me. My insides twisted. "Just ... ignore me. Start with your practice."

Clearing his throat, Artan faced the kids. "Right. Let's start."

The class started and I hadn't expected it to be so simple. Knowing tziganes, I thought these kids would hold the swords skillfully and move like masters. But Artan started by reminding them of the proper stances, the way to hold the sword, how to swing it without losing the grip, and other basic stuff.

I had no idea why Artan was in charge of this class because I could easily see how tense—or tenser—he was getting with each passing minute. His steps as he walked around the students were heavy, his sharp jaw ticked with annoyance, and he kept pressing his lips into a thin line as if swallowing back curses.

For the next exercise, Artan showed them how to swing the sword while advancing, without losing their stance and balance. Then he went around the kids, observing as they performed the same move and correcting them if necessary.

Looking like he barely could hold his sword right, Paddy tripped on his own feet and fell on his knees. His sword skidded across the mat, bumping into the feet of another boy, who lost his balance, but was able to stay up.

That didn't stop him from glaring at Paddy. "Pay attention, worm," the boy whispered, too low for Artan, who was on the other side to the room, to hear.

However, Artan wasn't in a good mood either. Upon seeing the scene, he marched toward Paddy.

"Seriously, what the hell—"

"It's okay," I said out loud, stepping inside the room. I couldn't let Artan reprimand the poor boy like that. Perhaps he didn't have experience teaching kids, but I did, and being mean to them and instilling fear into them, wasn't the way. After picking up the fallen sword, I stood beside Paddy and fixed my eyes on Artan's, trying to match his harsh posture. "I can help him."

Skeptical, Artan simply crossed his arms and said, "Go ahead."

I wouldn't cave in front of him. Instead, I filled my core with resolve and ignored him. Using the eye-level technique, I knelt down beside Paddy and smiled softly at him. "It's okay, Paddy. We all make mistakes. You know who I am, right?"

His eyes bugged, he nodded his head. "The heart maiden."

"That's right. Besides magic training, I also train in combat with Artan, and let me tell you, I'm terrible at it." I widened my smile, trying to put him at ease. His eyes and shoulders relaxed just a little bit. "I keep messing up, but you know what's more important when training?" He shook his head. "Not giving up." I stood and got closer to him. I handed him the sword, but instead of letting go, I adjusted his grip. There wasn't much I could do with his little hand and thick hilt, but as long as I brought a little confidence into him, it would work. "I bet you already heard this, but think of the sword as an extension of your arm." I drew his arm out, extending it in front of him. "And anchor your feet firm on the ground. Distribute your weight on both legs. This way, you have a solid base and won't fall that easily."

The boy adjusted his stance, widening his feet and sinking lower. "Like this?"

I glanced to Artan. He dipped his chin once. A proud smile spread across my lips, and I turned back to Paddy. "Just like that. Now, keep that in mind and do it again."

I stepped back and watched as Paddy, probably feeling a little more confident, executed the move with precision.

Artan stepped to my side and raised an eyebrow at me. "I thought you weren't paying attention to our sessions," he said in a low voice.

I rolled my eyes. "I'm always paying attention, but that doesn't mean I suddenly can do it all."

One corner of his lips tugged up, but only for a moment. Then his brows slammed down again and he turned to the other children. "All right. Next move."

In the end, I stayed by Paddy during the entire class. Occasionally, I helped other kids too, but just because they wanted some attention from the heart maiden.

An hour after the session had started, Artan dismissed the kids. Most just threw their swords down and ran out the door. Artan started screaming at them to come back and put the swords away.

"They are gone, Artan," I said, picking the nearest practice sword from the floor. "Next time, tell them they have to clean up after themselves *before* you dismiss them."

He grumbled some curses under his breath, but helped me pick up the swords from the mat.

After we dropped them in the wooden box in the corner of the room, Artan turned to me. Those amber eyes were too intense for this early in the morning. "Thank you."

I frowned, sensing some kind of trick here. "For?"

"Helping."

I stared at him, confused. Artan was thanking me for helping him. Where was my cell phone? I needed to record this. "I think I heard you wrong." I pretended to rub my ear, as if it was clogged.

His half-smile was back. "No, you heard it right. But don't get used to it."

I grinned. "Ah, just when I thought we were bonding." I meant it as a joke, but then his smile was gone and the shine in his eyes became two molten embers. Heat spread over my cheeks. "I mean ..."

"I know what you mean."

I tilted my head at him. "Can I ask a question?"

"If I say no, you won't ask?"

Did he know me that well? "If you get so frustrated teaching kids, why do you do it?"

His jaw ticked. "Sloan usually teaches the younger kids. I get the teenagers. But he's busy this morning, so I had to step in."

"Ah, that makes sense."

"But you're right. As much as I think it's important, I don't have the patience to teach kids."

"Well, it's not like you have a lot of patience teaching me either."

The lopsided grin was back. "Let's just say you can be as difficult as the little kids are."

I rolled my eyes again. "But I'm prettier." Again, another joke that came out wrong. What the hell was I doing.

Clearing his throat, Artan marched away as if I had burned him.

I stared at his back while he walked around the mat, picking up what? Lint? Was lint so much more interesting than me?

Why did I care about that? Even if I found him to be a fine specimen, he was out of limits. I was out of limits. After all, I was the damned heart maiden. I wasn't to be touched. And with his gigantic honor, Artan would be the last man on earth to lay a hand on me.

I sighed.

Surprising me, Artan suddenly turned to me, his brows curled down. "Don't you have magic training this morning?"

I gasped. "Shit!" I picked up my phone from my pocket and checked the time. I was only forty minutes late. "Shit, shit, shit. Your grandmother will kill me."

"Just tell her you were practicing with me," he said, his voice softening. "I'll take responsibility for that."

My heart skipped a beat at that. He would do that for me? "Thanks," I whispered.

"Now go before she skins us both alive."

"Right."

I ran out of the room, out the building, and down the hill, all the while with a smile on my lips. Why did I look like a silly dummy? Because Artan had been kind to me for the first time? That was ridiculous.

Before I could dwell on Artan and his kindness, I turned the corner and bumped into two warriors.

"There you are!" one said, reaching toward me. His hand fell short, but the way he looked over me with pinched brows, turned my stomach. "Are you all right?"

"Y-yes," I said. I wanted to be nice and call him by name, but truth be told, I didn't know most of the warriors' names. "I was training with Artan and lost track of time."

The other warrior hissed. "Darcy was going out of her mind thinking something had happened to you. All warriors are out, looking for you inside and outside the enclave."

Shit. "I'm sorry, I muttered.

"Let's go," the first warrior said, his tone harsh. "Darcy is waiting for you."

The feeling that I was a prisoner in a golden jail hit me hard in the chest just then. I let out a defeated breath, and with my tail between my legs, I followed the warriors to the old hag's house.

8

I DIDN'T HAVE ANY DAYS OFF, NOT EVEN WEEKENDS. WAKING UP early on a Saturday to train magic with the old hag was really a bad way to start my weekend—not that I was having any restful nights lately. I had been waking up too early for weeks now, but now I couldn't even stay in bed and stare at the ceiling for a moment longer.

However, my morning got much better when I was walking down the streets from my house to Darcy's.

I heard the claps and stomps before I saw them. A smile stretched over my lips when I turned the corner and saw kids dancing flamenco right in the middle of one of the narrow streets, right between two houses. Five girls and four boys, all tapping their feet and clapping their hands, moving their hips and arms along with the beat they created.

My heart squeezed.

It had been only Wednesday when I had to give up dance —because of the safety of others around me, not because of my own—and it already felt like I had let it go eons ago. My stomach sank. Damn, I missed it so much.

The kids saw me approaching and stopped dancing. Some of them, the oldest ones, bowed their heads at me.

Ugh.

"No, don't stop," I told them. "Please, keep dancing." They exchanged unsure glances. I saw a girl of about ten who had a pair of castanets. She hadn't been playing them a few moments ago. I snatched the castanets from her. "Here, I'll join you." I started playing the castanets, and stomping my foot, and moving my hips. The little ones, who couldn't be older than five, joined me instantly.

Dancing was contagious and soon all the kids danced with me.

Their energy filled me with a pure, content feeling, emboldening me and giving me strength. To what, I didn't know. Anything fate decided to throw in my face, perhaps. Right now, right in that moment, while I tapped the castanets and stomped my feet, and rolled my hips, I felt like there was nothing I couldn't take on.

"What are you doing?"

I gasped and turned toward the voice.

Theron stood a few feet away, his eyes narrowed at me.

The kids stopped playing and huddled behind me.

"I-I was dancing with the kids," I explained, as if he hadn't seen me. The heating, overwhelming feeling that had been pulsing inside me faded, and I was left with the warmth of the flower's call, teasing and taunting me. Making me miserable again. I handed the castanets to the girl and took two steps toward Theron. Now that he had free access to Lovell because of me, he was here almost all the time. "How about you? I wasn't expecting you until later this afternoon, for our sparring session."

"There wasn't much to do at Bellville, so I decided to

come early." His tone was harsher than usual and his posture straighter. He glanced behind me, to the kids that now ran down the street, probably uncomfortable with the mean warrior from the other enclave. "Shouldn't you be training?"

I rolled my eyes. "My next lesson starts in a few minutes." Shit. I had to hurry. I walked past him, knowing he would follow me.

A second later, he was by my side, keeping pace with me. "How long have you been awake?"

"A little over an hour, I think."

His dark eyes narrowed. "You could have been training."

I stopped dead in my tracks. "I've been training twelve to fourteen hours a day, and I've been sleeping poorly." Plagued with body and mind aches and nightmares of me never finding the damn heart flower. "I need some time to relax."

"We don't have time to relax."

"I'm not a machine, Theron! I can't keep going nonstop. I'll break."

"I know, I know, but ..." He pressed his lips into a thin line.

I buried my hands on my hips. "But what?"

He let out a long breath. "All right, I'll be breaking some rules here, but come with me."

Taking me by surprise, Theron grabbed my hand and pulled me in the opposite direction—toward the center of the enclave, where the main square and main buildings were. At this time of the morning, a couple of people were already bustling around. They all stopped and acknowledged me, either by waving or bowing, as we walked past them.

"Where are you taking me?" I asked Theron, not really concerned, but curious.

"Here." He walked to the infirmary and pushed the front door open. "Go in and see for yourself."

My brows furrowed. Slowly, I crossed the threshold and entered the infirmary. I found myself in a reception room with some couches and chairs and a small desk to the corner and two doors beside it. And tziganes filling up the space. All the couches and chairs were taken, and there was no one behind the desk.

A teenager saw me coming in. She elbowed a woman to her side, who widened her eyes at me. In turn, she leaned over another young woman and whispered something to her, making her glance my way. In a matter of seconds, everyone in the room turned to me.

"What's going on?" I asked Theron in a low voice.

He stood behind me like a mute pillar.

One little boy walked up to me and tugged on my jeans. "Are you here to heal them?"

"I ... heal ... what?" I was even more confused. I glanced over my shoulder at Theron.

Without a word, he grabbed my elbow and dragged me across the room. He opened one of the doors and pushed me in.

I gasped and my knees wobbled.

"Oh my ..."

I had been here before, after I had punched Artan's shoulder during practice and broken my fingers. Well, I hadn't broken them, but the pain that I felt, and the way I couldn't move them for a couple of days, Artan had brought me over and the healer—not Darcy, thankfully—had taken me to the back room, which was simply a wide, long room with twenty cots or so and curtains to separate the spaces. At the time, it had been me and an older woman who had come in because of a cold.

Now ... now the place was packed. All the cots were taken and there were more tziganes, visibly sick, occupying chairs along the walls. Healers, or probably helpers since I doubted there were that many healers in Lovell, ran around the room, tending to the people.

"What's going on?" I asked again, my voice weak.

"We were instructed to not let you know about this yet, but—"

"What are you doing here?" Ryane appeared in front of me. Artan's younger sister had her hair tied back in a tight bun and she was carrying rags in her gloved hands. She glared at Theron. "She isn't supposed to be here."

"It's time she knows," he said, firm.

"Know what?" I croaked, still having difficulty talking.

Ryane shook her head and turned away.

I took a large step back and leaned against the wall, needing some support. "Theron, spill." His brows slammed down. "You brought me here, damn it, now you tell me what's going on."

"His orders were to keep you away from here." Darcy emerged from the crowd, followed by Ryane, who probably went to get her grandmother. She wiped her hands on a white towel, then turned her cold eyes to me. "But, since you're here now, I'll tell you." She gestured to the people behind her. "These are the sick tziganes."

"Sick?" I asked, already knowing the answer, but needing to hear it out loud.

"Yes, Mirella. These are the tziganes who are becoming increasingly sicker because they haven't had a dose of the elixir from the heart flower in a long time."

"But …" I looked around. "You said a few. Only a few tziganes had fallen ill."

"I never said that." She paused. "What? You thought getting sick with the heart disease is like a simple cold?" I didn't know what to say to that. "I told you before. The heart diseases can be deadly."

"No …"

When they had told me some tziganes were ill, I hadn't imagined much. I had really imagined they had some bad case of seasonal allergies and needed some rest and a good, strong dose of Claritin to feel better.

But this … this was much worse.

Little kids to seniors, all coughing their lungs out, and with sickly gray skin tone, and damp hair, as if they had a high fever and were sweating it out. Stunned, I walked to the back of the room, trying to absorb everything. Toward the back, the curtains were closed.

I reached my hand to open it, but Darcy snatched it away. "Don't. You don't want to see how these ones are."

My stomach sank. "Are they going to die?" Darcy stared at me, no answer. "Will all of them die?" I repeated the question, raising my voice.

Some eyes turned to us, mostly healers and helpers who were conscious enough to understand us.

"Eventually, yes."

I sucked in a sharp breath. "There's nothing else that can heal them? The only thing is …"

Darcy nodded. "The elixir from the heart flower, yes."

I already knew that, but I had hoped she would say there was something else. Some other elixir that could at least help in the meantime.

I glanced around some more, letting the reality of it all

sink in. If I didn't follow the flower, if I didn't figure out how to follow the flower, all these people might die. Would die.

Facing Darcy, I asked, "Why didn't you tell me before?"

"We almost did, but Artan interceded on your behalf."

I frowned. "Why?"

"He said it would interfere with your training. You would be too worried about the people and, instead of helping you focus, it would upset you and you wouldn't make any progress." Not that I had made any progress anyway, but he was right. If I had known, I wouldn't have focused on training at all. That was actually thoughtful of him. "Of course, some of us were against it, but my grandson can be persuasive when he wants to."

Which didn't make any sense. I thought Artan was siding with his grandmother in the push-Mirella-until-we-break-her routine.

To my right, an older man started a loud coughing fit, and to my left, a little girl started crying, asking for her mother.

I swallowed the terror building in my throat, but all I did was force it into my chest instead. "Is it contagious?"

"No."

"So why can't this girl's mother be with her?"

Darcy gestured to a cot farther along the wall. "That's her mother. And between them is her older brother."

The terror expanded in my chest, and this time, I couldn't contain it. I let out a loud whimper, then marched to the little girl. As the heart maiden, there had to be something I could do.

"Hi, sweet bun," I said, taking her hand in mine.

Her cries faded and she blinked, staring at the ceiling as if she couldn't see anything. "*Dai?*"

I knelt beside her bed, still holding her hand tight. "No, sweet bun, it's Mirella."

"Mi-Mirella, the heart maiden?"

"Yes, that's me."

"You're here." She gasped, her eyes darting side to side, as if looking for me, but still not seeing me. "That means ... did you find the flower?"

A punch to the gut.

I inhaled deeply as tears burned the back of my eyes. "Not yet, but I will."

"Oh." The girl's arm slacked, as if my statement had been too much for her and now she had given up.

Still holding on to her hand, I focused on my magic. I tried calling it forth, hoping it would fill my veins and push my energy. I should be able to heal them. I had to.

I called and called, but with my panic and frustration, my magic only flickered in the back of whatever chest it liked to be locked in.

The girl yelped and jerked my hand from hers.

I shot up, realizing my magic, my fire, had warmed my hand, making it too hot for contact. With wide eyes, I stared at the tender redness in the little girl's palm.

Oh my God, I had done that.

The little girl started crying again. Wailing. Sobbing.

And I ran out of the infirmary.

"Mirella, wait," Theron called me once we were out in the square. I didn't stop. Faster than me, he sprinted and put himself in my way. I slammed into him, bouncing back, but he grasped my arms and kept me up.

"Let me go," I shouted.

He did, but he didn't back up. "I only wanted to help. I thought if you saw how many of your people need you—"

"That didn't help at all." A sob escaped my throat, but I was able to keep the tears back. "I need ... I need a minute. Tell Darcy we'll start our training a little later today."

Averting my gaze, I walked past him. I thought he was going to stop me again, or follow me into my house, but thankfully, he stayed behind.

I slammed the front door closed and leaned into it.

"Mirella? Is that you?" my mother called from the other side of the house.

"Yes," I forced out.

Smiling, she appeared behind the kitchen's archway. "Breakfast is almost ready." Her smile fell away. "What's wrong?"

"Nothing." She coughed and my eyes bulged. "Are you okay?"

"Yes, why?"

"You coughed."

"I had something in my throat. I'm fine." She tilted her head. "How about you, *chey*?"

"I'm fine," I snapped before rushing up the stairs.

"What about breakfast?"

"I'm not hungry!"

I fled into my bedroom and closed the door.

This was too much, too fast. It hadn't been a month since I found out I was the heart maiden. I needed more time to train, to learn, to get used to it.

Did a heart maiden need time to learn what she was born to do? Didn't she just know? Just got it done?

Perhaps I wasn't the heart maiden. Perhaps Lovell and Bellville were mistaken. Perhaps Annie played us all. But, even if she was the heart maiden, she was a little girl. She wouldn't understand what was going on and why the tziganes needed her. I couldn't throw her under the train like that.

Or perhaps it was someone else entirely. Or there was no one. It had been all a mistake.

A sudden thought popped in my head and I lunged at my closet, looking for that lost item. I had completely forgotten I had it. I pulled the shoe box from the top shelf and knelt on the floor, putting the box down in front of me.

With trembling hands, I opened the lid. There. There was the heart flower that had been left on my doorstep a couple of months ago. I didn't know why I hadn't shown it to anyone or why I hadn't remembered it existed until now. I reached for it, hope blooming in my chest. This flower. We could use this flower to make the elixir.

But when I turned it around and examined the center, my heart wilted. The bud in the center, where the magic that spread to its petals and leaves was gone. Whoever gave me this flower had plucked the magic away first.

Feeling like a failure, I shoved the flower back into the shoe box and stayed in my locked room all day. I didn't open the door for anyone. Not for my mother when she came with food. Not for Theron and Artan begging me to train with them. Not for Ryane and Cora, who claimed they wanted to talk.

And, the more time I stayed in here alone with my thoughts, the surer I was of my decision.

I was leaving the enclave tonight.

9

I WAITED UNTIL NIGHT, UNTIL MY MOTHER WENT TO BED—OR tried to since I knew from her frantic knocks at my door that she was distraught over my isolation—then changed into all black and tiptoed to the kitchen downstairs.

I waited by the back door and watched my phone for the time.

Ten ...

Seven ...

Four ...

One ...

Midnight.

As I had come to know from not sleeping well, warriors patrolled the streets of the enclave and, right at midnight, two of them walked by the street behind our backyard. And there they were ... two warriors clad in their uniform —brown suede pants and vest, a beige shirt underneath, and leather boots and a belt around their waists with their sword hanging from it—walked past. As usual, they stopped, looked up the house, glanced all around, and only after making sure everything was okay, they moved on.

Another patrol would come around in an hour, and because of that, I couldn't waste time.

I gave the warriors ten minutes, enough time for them to reach the end of the street, turn right, and start down another one. Then, as silent as I could be, I opened the back door and ran from my new prison.

Since I didn't know the routes of the other patrols, I stayed in the shadows offered by the buildings and houses in case I needed to hide.

Besides seeing them crossing streets ahead of me, I hadn't encountered any on my path … until I got to the back gate, where five warriors were stationed.

I cursed. I knew I would have to face some warriors. Other than crossing through the gates, there was no way out of the enclave. Not even the forest was an option since it extended for miles and was surrounded by deep valleys and rivers—and I would probably get lost.

My first thought was to enter their minds and make them act like zombies for the few minutes it took me to open the gate and escape, but I had to be realistic here. I wasn't that good with my powers, not yet, and I probably couldn't control more than two or three tziganes at a time, and only if it was easy to enter their minds.

So I started on plan B.

Pretty terracotta flowerpots stood at the corners of almost every street, holding colorful flowers, or small trees, or fluffy bushes. I located the nearest one and rested my hand over a bunch of leaves. Closing my eyes, I focused on my weak magic and, hating myself for it, called on the fire within me. My palm heated up. Because the fire was part of me, I didn't feel it, but my hand turned orange and the leaves caught on fire.

I retreated to the shadows on the other side of the street as the fire spread.

Two of the guards turned in that direction. They sniffed the air.

"What's that?" one asked.

"It smells like smoke," another said.

A third joined them. "Fire. It could be a fire."

The three of them rushed down the street toward the burning flowerpot. Without wasting time, I poked into the remaining guards' minds. To my surprise, these two were either weak at protecting their minds, or they weren't expecting someone to take them over. Either way, it was too easy for me to push my powers in and force them to open the gates for me.

In less than a minute, I was out of the gates and running. I kept control of the guards until they had locked the gates again, and had forgotten they had opened it.

A thrill surged in my stomach and I felt exhilarated. Holy shit, what had I done? Manipulated warriors, controlled them, and escaped a heavily guarded enclave. It felt wrong and exciting at the same time.

I ran down the hidden path, and finally turned onto the back road that eventually led to the interstate. Just as we had agreed, Ellie was waiting for me in her car half a mile down the road.

I slipped into her car and embraced her. "Thanks for coming."

"Sure," she said. She pulled back and frowned at me. Her strawberry blond curls were disheveled as if she had gone to bed earlier and woke up in a rush to come pick me up, though we had agreed to this in the middle of the afternoon, and her blue eyes stared at me with concern. "Though I'm curious. What is going on? Why did you want a getaway ride at this hour?"

"Drive and I'll tell you all on the way."

As she drove to Broken Hill, I told her everything. From the intense training sessions, the juggling with dance and college, the pressure from the elder council to find the heart flower, then the alchemist and the revenant attacks, the call from the flower that I couldn't follow, my sudden move to Lovell and being forced to drop my classes and dance, and finally about the sick tziganes.

By the end of my speech, my eyes were wet and my voice broke.

Ellie parked the car in her spot in the parking lot beside her dorm building and reached over, taking my hands in hers.

"I understand, Mi," she said, her tone caring and careful. "It's too much, too fast."

"Exactly." I snorted. "God, I want to help but I don't know how."

She embraced me again. "We'll figure it out. Don't worry. But first, you need a big ass mug of hot tea and some rest."

I chuckled. "Now you sound like my mother."

She offered me a small smile. "Well, I think that means I'm wise."

"I wish."

She tugged on my hand. "Come on."

I followed her inside her dorm. Her roommate was out at a party with her boyfriend, which meant she would be out all night, and I could have her bed. I sat down on the bed and pulled my feet up, folding them underneath me. A minute later, Ellie handed me a fuming tea mug and sat beside me.

"You want to tell me more about it?" she asked.

"Enough about me," I said, trying to push the bad feelings aside. "We haven't had much time together. How is it going with you?"

Ellie shrugged. "Compared to tziganes, my life is boring. I don't do much; you know that. Classes, dance, having lunch with Tonia and Raul and some other people here, studying for midterms, partying a little. We had plans of going to Muévete last night, but Raul had to cancel. Just the normal stuff."

A pang cut through my heart, and I was sure the pain was visible in my expression. There was nothing I could do to hide the jealousy that suddenly consumed me.

"That sounds wonderful actually."

"Oh, Mi ... I didn't mean ... Shit, I didn't think before saying ..." She paused. "Your life is so amazing, Mi. You have to know that. Come on, who wouldn't love to live an adventure with hot, badass warriors and powerful magic?"

"I know it sounds cool, but once your life is always in danger, it isn't fun anymore."

"I get it." She paused, then repeated her previous question. "You want to talk more about it?"

I took a sip from the hot liquid and almost burned my tongue. "I don't know."

Ellie puckered her lips. "Hm, so ... this calling from the flower. What is it exactly?"

"I ... it's what I already told you. It's a warm feeling inside my chest, around my heart. There's no way of explaining it, and I know it's the heart flower. Besides, when I focus on it, I can smell them."

"But you can't follow the smell." It wasn't a question.

I sighed. "I wish."

"It's okay. We'll figure it out."

"What if I don't want to figure out?"

Ellie narrowed her eyes at me. "What do you mean?"

"I'm not sure the elder council is right. I think I might not be the heart maiden, and even if I am, I'm terrible at it. They need a new one."

"And how would they do that?"

I shrugged. "I don't know, but I imagine I can't be there for a new one to show up."

"What are you saying?"

I looked into her eyes, so she could see how serious I was. "I'm not sure I'll go back to Lovell."

Ellie gasped. "You're planning on running away?"

"Something like that …"

"Mi, when you said you needed a break from the enclave and asked to spend the rest of the weekend here, I didn't think you would be running away."

"Is that a problem? Wouldn't you have helped me if I had said anything?"

"No, I mean, I would, but I would have tried convincing you not to run away first."

I shot to my feet. The remainder of the tea sloshed around the mug, almost spilling over. "I thought you were on my side."

She stood in front of me. "I am on your side. Believe me. I just think you're too stressed out to see anything clearly." She put a hand on my shoulder. "I mean it. Why don't you go to sleep and rest, really rest? And tomorrow we can talk more about this. I'm sure you'll have another idea about this then."

As I crawled into bed, all I could think was that she was

wrong. Sleep would help because I needed rest. Despite not training all day, I was still a wreck—emotionally and physically. But sleep wouldn't change my mind.

Once more, I barely slept all night. My dreams were plagued with visions of the sick tziganes dying and coming back as zombies, coming after me and cursing me for not being able to save them. Among them, I saw Theron, Artan, Cora, and even little Annie.

Tired of trying to sleep only to end up jerking awake in terror, I sat up on Ellie's roommate's bed and started playing with my phone at four in the morning. I scrolled through social media. After a minute or two, even that made me feel bad and jealous and frustrated. Because alchemists could track me through whatever I wrote or a picture I posted, I was also forbidden from being active on social media, so all I could do was check on the people I knew without commenting or posting anything.

Angry, I closed the app and deleted all of them from my phone.

If I was going to run, it was better if I stayed off social media.

I sighed.

Was I going to run away?

I didn't know. I should since I didn't feel I was fit to be the heart maiden. Even if the council and the enclaves were right and I was the real heart maiden, I was doing nothing useful other than making them more upset and wasting their time trying to train me when they should be caring for the sick people.

But ... I also felt like I was doing something wrong, like I would disappoint my mother, and Theron, and Artan.

Ugh, this situation was impossible. I wanted to close my

eyes and go to sleep, sans nightmare, and when I woke up, I wanted to be a normal girl.

Was that too much to ask?

I glanced at the other bed across the small bedroom. Ellie looked so peaceful, hugging her pillow while sleeping. She was a simple human and I envied her for that.

A floorboard creaked outside the room's door and I sat up, my back straight. It was probably a student coming in late from some party, but with my nerves on edge, I couldn't dismiss it.

Instead, I scooted to the edge of the bed and watched the door and the light streaming from underneath it. My heart sped up as a shadow appeared beyond. The shadow kept moving, and I exhaled a relieved breath once the person was gone.

The floorboard creaked again and the shadow came back, stopping right in front of the door.

My heart jumped to my throat, and I jumped out of bed.

"Ellie," I whispered, calling her. "Ellie, there's someone here."

She mumbled something, but as the shadow didn't move, I went to the little kitchenette area and grabbed a big knife.

Sweat beaded on my forehead and I gripped the knife tight.

The lock clicked and the door swung open.

I charged the intruder.

10

I THREW MY ARM, AIMING FOR THE INTRUDER'S CHEST, BUT HE put his arm up, blocking my strike easily. Then, he twisted his hand and grabbed my wrist, bending my hand until my grip around the knife loosened. I yelped when he caught the knife, sure he would plunge it into my chest. Instead, he stabbed it into the kitchen's wooden counter beside him. The knife wobbled, but stayed up.

He tugged me closer, and I opened my mouth to yell. His free hand landed on top of my mouth.

"It's okay. It's me."

My eyes bulged and I let my gaze settle on his face. My eyes adjusted to the darkness and then I could see his features. Sharp angles, full lips, and meaningful eyes.

"Artan," I mumbled against his hand.

Letting go of me, he closed the door behind him. A second later, he was hovering over me again. I retreated, afraid of the harsh expression on his handsome face.

"What are you doing?" he asked, advancing on me. His

tone was tight, and I was sure he was struggling not to shout at me.

"I-I needed a break." I bumped against the window and Artan still loomed over me. The light coming from the moon and the streetlamps filtered through the glass, illuminating half of his face.

Had Darcy been lying about Artan interceding for me and trying to help me earlier? Because, from the murderous glint in his amber eyes, I couldn't imagine him ever defending me.

"A break?" He ran a hand through his hair, disheveling it some more. "I didn't want you to see the sick tziganes so soon, because I knew that would affect your training, but running away? I didn't think you would do that."

"What's going on?" Ellie sat up on her bed, rubbing the sleep from her eyes. When her gaze fell on Artan, her eyes widened. "What are you doing here?"

"I came to pick up a runaway girl," he said, not taking his eyes off me.

Ellie stood and puffed her chest. If the situation weren't delicate, it would have been funny—her small size in pajamas beside tall and strong Artan and his weapons.

"You're not taking her."

Slowly, he turned his face and glared at her. "Stay out of this."

"This is my room, my home at the moment, and you'll do what I say. If Mirella wants to stay, you'll go away and leave her be."

He gritted his teeth. "You—"

I gripped his arm and he returned his eyes to me. I dropped my hands and hid them behind me, but kept my head high. "She's just being a good friend. Please, leave her alone."

Artan groaned. "Can we continue this conversation in private?"

Ellie's room was a small square with only two doors: a small closet and a bathroom. I didn't want to go into the bathroom with him, and knowing our conversation would get heated, I didn't want to go to the hallway and risk waking up other students. I glanced out the window. Was he suggesting we went outside to talk?

There was only one other option. "We can go to the lobby, I guess."

Ellie sighed. "You two can stay right there. I need to go to the bathroom anyway." With a huff, she shuffled her feet and disappeared inside the bathroom.

A small smile adorned my lips. She looked like a tiny pixie taking on a huge troll, and it was all because she was my friend. I loved her for that.

"What are you smiling about?" Artan asked. He finally took a step back, giving me some room.

I folded my arms, suddenly conscious that I was wearing a thin sleeping tee and shorts—and no bra. "Nothing," I snapped.

Artan took a deep breath and his shoulders relaxed. His eyes softened. "Look ... I can't possibly pretend to know how it feels to have all this pressure and stress on you. I wish I could help you. I wish I could take some of this from you, I swear, but besides protecting you at all times, there's nothing more I can do." He paused. "But I can't protect you when you run away."

"I wasn't thinking ..." I confessed, realizing I did that a lot. I just acted, without thinking, which always made everything worse. "I just needed to get away. I was suffocating there and I felt like I would break if I stayed there any longer."

"Mirella ..." He said my name in such a tender way that it sent a shiver down my spine. "The enclave is your home now. You shouldn't feel suffocated there."

I snorted. "And how do you think I feel when I have this sensation—" I put my hand over my chest. "—this calling in here and I don't know what to do about it? I can feel the flower calling me, wanting me to find it, but I can't." Tears burned the back of my eyes. "And all those people are sick and dying because I can't follow this damn call. I can't stay there and simply watch them die." A hollow sob escaped my throat.

"Hey, hey." With one large step, Artan was right in front of me. His arms wrapped around my waist and he pulled me against him. I stiffened, trying not to think I was leaning against his hard chest, but it was impossible with my nose pressed right below his collarbone and his woody and leather scent invading my nostrils and derailing my thoughts. He held me tight, one hand running down my long, messy hair. "It's okay. Everything will be okay. We can figure this out ... together. We can go back home and I will talk to my *puri daj* and Sheila. Maybe having a different magic instructor will help. And we won't give up until you can answer the flower's call." He pulled back, one corner of his lips curled up. "Deal?"

The words got stuck in my throat as I stared into his amber eyes, lost in them and in the fact that he was still holding me near, his full lips so close to mine.

His cocky grin faded and the glint in his eyes changed. It became deeper, darker.

"I—"

A door creaked open and Artan jumped three feet back.

At first, I thought it was Ellie coming back from the bathroom, but it was Theron, marching into the room with the posture of a warrior.

His dark eyes darted from Artan to me, and back to Artan. "We need to go now."

There was something off about him. "What's going on?"

"We've found you; now we're taking you back," he said, a bite to his words.

I put my hands on my hips. "Theron, what's going on?"

He shook his head once, then glanced around. His gaze stopped for two seconds on Ellie, who was leaning against the bathroom door. I hadn't even seen her come back. Then, he fixed his attention on Artan as if trying to tell him something.

And apparently, Artan understood.

"We should go," Artan said, beckoning me to the door.

I didn't move. "Are you two communicating inside your heads?"

"We can't do that," Artan said, as if that was obvious.

"Then what is it?" I insisted. Theron and Artan exchanged another pained look. "I'm not moving until one of you tell me what is going on?"

Sighing, Theron turned his gaze to me. "It's your mother."

My throat went dry. "What about her?"

"She's sick."

11

I LOST MY LEGS RUNNING INTO MY HOUSE. I TRIPPED ON THE stairs, fell on my knees. Artan and Theron shot forward to help me up, but I waved them off and pushed up myself. As if I hadn't banged my knees against the hardwood, I continued taking the steps two by two until I reached the second floor landing.

Then I halted by the closed suite's door, afraid of going in. In my mind, I conjured an image of my mother, annoying and lively as always but with a mild cold. That was all this was. Nothing more. It couldn't be anything more.

A heavy hand landed on my shoulder. "We're here for you," Artan said.

"I know," I said, and for the first time, I felt good about that. Reassured. Artan and Theron and Ellie, who had insisted on coming with us, had become strong pillars in my life, the people I could depend on. My friends. Even if some of them—namely Theron and Artan—could be more pricks than friends. But I knew they were annoyingly protective because they cared.

"We'll stay here," Ellie said from behind. "Call us if you need anything."

Taking a deep breath, I opened my mother's bedroom door and stepped in.

The air fled my lungs.

My mother and I had a delicate relationship. We had never been friends, and for the last fifteen, sixteen months, we had become real strangers. When I was younger, I had been ashamed of her and her odd ways and her overprotective side. It was only recently, when she emerged back in my life, that I understood all she did to protect me.

Our relationship might not be the best, but she was still my mother and I still loved her, which was why I wasn't ready to see her like this.

My mother, the strong and brave Marisa, was lying in her bed, her long dark curls a mess atop her head, sweat beading her face, her lips parched, her eyes sunk in ... and little black spots all over her bare arms.

"Mirella," she whispered, her voice weak, when she saw me.

Tears filled my eyes and I approached the bed. She lifted her trembling hand, and I gripped it firmly. "You lied to me. When I asked you yesterday morning if you were sick, you lied to me."

"I didn't want to worry you."

"Well, I'm worried."

"Sorry, I didn't think it would take over so fast."

I breathed in, forcing the tears back. "How long have you known?"

"A few days," she confessed. "Like I said, it was supposed to be slower." She gasped, as if it was too hard to breathe.

I touched my free hand to her forehead. "You're burning

up." I let go of her hand and went to her bathroom, where I got a small washcloth, wetted it, then came back and put it on her forehead. She exhaled deeply, savoring the coolness from the cold water. I glanced around and saw medicine and elixirs on the nightstand. "You're here alone. You should be at the infirmary."

"There's no place there," she said. Another punch to my stomach. I wouldn't be able to take much more. "The healers are coming here every couple of hours to check on me."

"That's not enough."

My mother went quiet, and for a moment, it seemed like she wasn't even breathing. Desperation rose in me and I checked her pulse. Too slow for comfort, but steady.

I let out a long breath and a tear rolled down my face. This couldn't be happening. We had barely found each other again and were working on fixing our relationship. She couldn't leave me now.

I knelt beside the bed and rested my forehead on the mattress.

A hand caressed my hair. "It'll be okay, *chey*," my mother whispered.

I lifted my eyes to her. "I don't see how."

"I might know a way."

My spine straightened. "What do you mean?"

"Find Cianna. She lives in a cabin deep in the mountain, northwest of here, near a place called Hollow's Bane."

"What? Why? What can she do?"

My mother closed her eyes. "I think she has some spare elixir ..."

I gasped. "I don't understand. Who is this woman, and why would she have the elixir?"

"Just ... just find her," my mother whispered.

"Mom?"

She didn't answer. My heartbeat went up. I checked her pulse again. Still slow and steady. She was tired, sleeping.

I stared at her for a minute more before standing up and kissing her forehead. "I love you, Mom."

Then I gathered my thoughts and my courage and went to my friends.

I opened the door and found the three of them—Artan, Theron and Ellie—waiting for me.

I donned my heart maiden mantle and said, "We have a mission."

12

———

THE ELDER COUNCIL DIDN'T LIKE THAT I CALLED ANOTHER urgent meeting. At the moment, I couldn't care less what they thought, but since I was trying to help the entire enclave, not just my mother, I felt like I shouldn't step on anyone's toes and do things the right way.

And that meant asking the council for permission to go on my mission to find this woman named Cianna.

I stood before the council with Artan and Theron and Ellie behind me. As usual, Darcy started the meeting.

"Mirella, isn't that a *gadjo* standing behind you?" she asked, as if Ellie couldn't hear her.

I knew the council would skin me alive for bringing a human to the enclave, but I was done caring what Darcy and the council thought. "Yes, she's my friend."

"You know that's forbidden, dear."

"What are you going to do? Banish me?"

She gasped, visibly outraged by my words. "Who do you think you're talking to?"

"Look," I started, not wanting to waste time arguing with

her more than necessary. "We have a more important matter to discuss."

Darcy folded her hands over the table before her. "Oh, really? Are you still feeling the heart flower's call? Can you follow it?"

Touché. "I'm still feeling it, but no, I can't follow it."

"Then you're wasting *our* time. We should be helping the sick tziganes."

"I want to go after Cianna," I blurted out. For some reason, I thought Darcy knew that name.

Her eyes widened and some other members of the council gasped. Bingo.

"What do you want with her?" Oscar asked, his voice tight.

"My mother believes she has some spare flower elixir. I need to find her and ask her to lend me some." I thought lending instead of giving was a better choice. With a good elixir dose now, I could relax and train harder, so later I could follow the flower's call and make more elixir—then I would repay my debt.

The council members talked in hushed tones among themselves for a couple of minutes. My patience was wearing thin. We didn't have time to waste. I was here as a formality. If they said no, I was going to run away again. But this time, I knew Artan and Theron wouldn't stop me. They would go with me.

"All right," Darcy finally spoke up. "Assemble a small team and go. By my calculations, you have four days to be back with the elixir before your mother dies."

I winced at her callous words. Couldn't she have softened the blow? I really didn't like this old hag.

"Thank you," I said. Then, without another word, I pivoted and exited the room, my steps sure, my head high.

"What now?" Ellie asked in a low voice as we walked out of the building.

I glanced at her. "Now we gear up and go save everyone."

IT TOOK US A COUPLE OF HOURS TO GET READY, BUT SOON WE were on the road. Artan drove his dark blue SUV, I took the passenger seat, and Theron and Ellie shared the backseat.

I tried, I argued, I even shouted, but Ellie was as stubborn as they came. She wouldn't have it. Despite the reminder that she would miss classes and maybe some of her midterms, she stomped her foot and didn't back down. Theron and Artan also complained, but they soon noticed arguing with her would only take some of our precious time and get us nowhere.

There was another passenger in the SUV—Felix. As we were leaving Lovell, Sheila called saying Felix was going crazy in his cage. He was roaring and running and bumping against the metal bars, scratching the ground and scaring them all. She begged me to come see him, to try and calm him down. Since Bellville was only five miles from Lovell, I asked Artan to make a quick pit stop there.

As soon as he saw me, Felix stopped and projected his feelings in my head. He knew what we were doing, where we were going, and he wanted to come with me. He showed me he could take care of me, be my bodyguard as much as Theron and Artan, and he also showed he would break free of that cage somehow if I didn't agree.

So now the huge white lion occupied the SUV's trunk, snuggly.

After thirty minutes on the interstate, Artan took a dirt road that led deeper into the forest. After another fifteen minutes or so, he veered the SUV off the road.

"What are you doing?" I asked, holding on to the seat, afraid he would drive the car into an unseen ditch.

"No roads go near the base of the mountain. I'm taking us as close as we can get with the car, then we need to go on foot."

I glanced down to my clothes and shoes. I was glad Theron had insisted Ellie and I wear the warriors' uniforms with their thick boots and suede pants, otherwise I would have been wearing ripped jeans or high heeled boots for a trek in the woods. From our brief talk before we left the enclave, I knew it would take us a couple of days to get wherever we needed to go, but still, my mind hadn't registered how wild this adventure would be until Artan stopped the car when the trees became too close together and the bushes and roots too tall and thick for the SUV to get through.

Once out of the car, I stared out at the thick forest. From here, the canopy of the leafless tree branches was so close together, there was no way of seeing the mountain ahead. I gulped, realizing that this might not be a mission to retrieve the heart flower, but it was still my first mission as a heart maiden.

Artan appeared beside me, his eyes on the trees. "Ready?" He hiked the strap of his backpack over his shoulder.

I grabbed my bag from the SUV and sighed. "Ready as I'll ever be."

He locked the car—seemed unnecessary, but I guess I would have done the same—and then we set off.

Artan and Theron took the front, Ellie and I trailed behind them, and Felix followed us.

Two minutes into our journey, Ellie slipped over some roots, but regained her balance quickly.

Theron mumbled something.

Ellie grunted. "If you have a problem, say it to my face."

Theron spun around and I almost bumped into him. He glared at Ellie. "Yes, I have a problem. I don't care how much Mirella likes you, you're a *gadjo* and you shouldn't be here."

"But I am, so deal with it."

"Are you always this stubborn?"

"Is that—?"

"Hey, you two," I said, interrupting them. "Can you stop? We're just wasting time arguing about things we can't change right now."

Ellie crossed her arms. "Mi is right."

"Just because she's right, doesn't mean I agree with it," Theron said.

Oh my God, what was his problem?

Rolling my eyes, I walked past them. "Let's keep going," I told Artan.

One corner of his lips tugged up. "But it's almost entertaining."

I chuckled. "Yeah, for about three minutes. Then I'm sure I'll try to strangle one of them."

Artan and I marched a little faster, putting some distance between Ellie and Theron. Every five steps, I glanced over my shoulder to make sure they were coming. They were, but they hadn't stopped arguing yet. Behind them, Felix seemed like an obedient dog going for a stroll in the park.

I lifted my chin and inhaled deeply, enjoying the crisp air of the trees. It was refreshing and I felt almost energized—

until I turned my thoughts inward and remembered all that had happened the past couple of days. I felt the dull warmth of the heart flower around my heart, and my spirit deflated.

"Hey," Artan started, glancing at me. "It'll be okay. We'll find Cianna and we'll convince her to share her elixirs with us." He patted his backpack. "Or we can bribe her. I came prepared."

"Let's just hope she'll make it easy on us so we can get back fast."

The longer we delayed, the chances were that more tziganes would fall ill, and the already sick ones were going to be worse.

Artan nudged me with his elbow. "Your mother is in good hands. She'll hang on for as long as it takes."

I nodded. Before leaving the enclave, I had set up a schedule with Ryane and Cora. Ryane had to help at the infirmary, but she would go check on my mother at least three times a day. Meanwhile, Cora and Rye had moved in until I got back, so they could keep an eye on my mother in case she needed help between Ryane's visits.

"I hope she does," I finally said. "I know we're not exactly friends, but she's still my mother. I love her despite everything."

Artan reached over and took my hand in his. "I know." My insides froze and I stiffened, but Artan didn't seem to notice. "You have nothing to worry about. Your mother will be fine, and we'll find this woman and we'll get the elixirs. And when we get back, we'll train hard and figure out how you can follow the flower's call."

He turned his amber eyes to me.

Just then, a ray of sunshine broke through the trees, illuminating his whole face and setting his eyes alight into two golden flames.

By Saint Sara-la Kali, Artan was handsome. I had always known that, but every time I stopped and took the time to appreciate it, the air was knocked out of my lungs.

His eyes narrowed, and he pulled his hand away from mine. "Mirella, I—"

His words died as a shriek filled the air.

13

My heart went into overdrive as a woman with bark-like skin and Rapunzel-long black hair jumped out from the trees, right in front of Artan and me.

Artan put his arm out before me and took a large step back, pulling me with him.

"Muma Padurii," he muttered, resting his hand on the hilt of his sword.

"Muma what?" I asked, but he didn't answer me. His gaze was locked on the strange figure swaying before us.

The woman looked old and made of entwined tree branches, her skin dry and brownish gray, her limbs long, her fingers like thorns, her eyes dark and depthless. She peeled her thin lips back, revealing dark teeth.

"What are you doing in my forest?" she asked, her voice thin and shrill. Otherworldly.

Artan pushed back another step. "We don't mean to intrude, Muma. We just need to cross through to the mountains."

She hissed, swaying from one big, bare foot to another. A

gentle breeze blew, lifting the hem of her long dirty and shredded white dress, revealing long, hairy legs. Who was this woman? "You can only pass if I say so."

"What do you want?" Theron asked from right behind me. I hadn't seen him and Ellie approaching us.

She hissed again. "You cannot bribe with material things, tzigane. All I want is to protect my forest."

"Her forest?" I whispered to Artan.

"She's a forest protector," he said.

"A crazy one at that," Theron added.

Muma Padurii clicked her tongue and sniffed the air. "I can't believe it." She whipped her head to me, and I felt as if a demon were staring at me. She swayed forward, closer to us. "What do we have here?"

Artan gripped my wrist and pulled me back another foot. "If you know, then you know we've come in peace."

Muma Padurii snapped her teeth together and I winced. "In peace?" She turned her black eyes to me again. "Haven't you come for the flower? Plucking the flower from the ground is exactly the opposite of protecting my forest."

My eyes widened, my heart stuttered. "The flower is here? You know where it is?"

"You don't know?" She tilted her head at me. "Aren't you following its call?"

"No," I said too quickly. I didn't care if I looked desperate. I would kiss the ground this creature walked on if she took me to the heart flower. "I can feel it, but I can't follow it. I have no idea where it is."

She narrowed her eyes. "Then what are you doing here? Destroying my forest?"

"No, no," Artan said, his words calm, firm. "We need to cross the forest. That's all we want."

Felix appeared by my side and snarled at the strange woman.

She bared her teeth at him, then glance at me. "A heart maiden and a heart animal. How unusual."

"Please, Muma," Artan tried again.

Muma Padurii seemed to consider that. "I have a proposal."

"No, wait, you said you know where the flower is," I said. She couldn't drop that bomb and not tell me.

"Hear my proposal first, heart maiden." Her tone grew cold as she continued, "You will go through my forest and do whatever you have to do. But ... the heart maiden stays here. As insurance."

My heart skipped a beat. Stay here with this creature?

Felix snarled again and Artan's grip on my wrist tightened. "Hell, no."

"No? Then I'll make it more interesting," she said, showing off her dark teeth again. "You three go, the heart maiden stays. When you get back, I'll make sure my forest is intact. Once I confirm all is well, I'll take you to the heart flower."

I turned to Artan.

"You can't be considering this," he said.

"If it's the only way to get the flower ..."

"But—"

I screamed as something wrapped around my waist and legs and pulled me up.

"I think the heart maiden agrees with my proposal. Now off with you." Muma Padurii brought her hands up and long vines shot from behind tree trunks and the canopies and even the ground, chasing after Artan, Theron, Ellie, and Felix.

Soon, I was surrounded by moving branches and lost sight of my friends. Other than the grunts coming from the guys, the slash of metal on the vines, the growls from Felix, and the screams from Ellie, I had no idea how they were faring.

This Muma bitch was getting on my nerves.

I placed my hands on the vines around me and focused, channeling my magic. I called upon my fire. I made my skin red hot, but not enough to start a fire. I just needed to burn through the wood so I could get free.

It took a moment, but the wood crumbled underneath my touch, becoming ash.

I fell to the ground in all fours, jarring my arms and knees.

New vines came for me. Grunting, I pushed up and lifted my hands. The vines rushed at me and I knife-hand blocked them, purposefully touching them with my hot hands. They jerked back, but kept surrounding me.

"Guys?" I shouted. "Where are you?"

"Here!" I heard Ellie, a hint of panic in her voice.

The wall of vines moved and I saw Artan on the other side. "Are you okay?" he asked before slashing his sword at a long branch.

My breathing came in small gasps, my heart beat fast, I felt like screaming, but other than that, I was fine. "I think so."

"Theron!" Artan shouted.

"I'm here!" Theron shouted back from somewhere to our left.

"Cut through the vines," Artan ordered. "Get Ellie. Let's get out of here."

"Deal!" Theron answered.

Artan glanced at me. "When I say, you get down, okay?"

"Okay," I muttered.

He slashed his sword through the vines. Once, twice ... three time. "Now!"

I knelt on the ground and lowered my torso over my legs. A gust of wind blew over my head, whipping my hair around and pushing me back.

The vines and branches retreated, taken by the wind.

"You won't get away so easy!" the Muma Padurii shrieked, her voice echoing from everywhere.

"Run!" Artan shouted.

I jumped to my feet and ran, following his trail, and we put some distance between us and the vines. A dozen feet to my right, I saw Ellie and Theron, also running away. I veered to them, always pushing ahead, but wanting to get closer. Artan was right by my side.

I looked back, trying to find Felix. I could hear him growling and snarling, but I couldn't see him.

"Just keep running," Theron said.

A scream erupted through the forest, trembling the trees, shaking the ground. Ellie tripped, I leaned against a trunk, and the guys halted and tried to stay on their feet.

Vines exploded from the ground, separating us again.

"Run! Run!" one of the guys shouted.

My heart racing, my breathing shallow, I pushed from the trunk and ran.

The vines advanced toward us.

"Don't stop!"

I wasn't planning on it.

I ran and ran and ran. Every few seconds, I glanced back at the vines—and they kept coming.

I ran past a line of trees close together, then halted, my

breath knocked out of my lungs. I was at the edge of a deep valley. Unless I planned on rolling down to what looked like my death, or at least a few broken bones, I didn't have anywhere to go.

Preparing myself for the worst, I faced the trees, placed my feet apart, and raised my hands, heat coming off my palms in waves.

And I waited for the vines to come for me.

But they never did.

Slowly, I lowered my arms and stepped back through the trees. There was no vine or branch or root out of place. It was as if the crazy Muma Padurii had never sent anything after me.

After us.

Gasping, I glanced around.

Where were my friends?

14

P ANIC ROSE TO MY CHEST AND UP MY THROAT, THREATENING TO choke me.

Oh my God, what if Muma Padurii had them all?

Otherwise, why would she have stopped attacking?

Well, to be honest, I had no idea why she attacked us in the first place. We weren't doing anything to her forest, just walking through it.

My chest was tight as I looked around, searching for signs of my friends or Muma Padurii. I didn't want her to catch me unprepared.

I called on my power and held it close. Even though I still didn't know how to control it—and I had taken a little bit of my mother's suppressing elixir before leaving, just in case—I felt more comfortable walking around alone in a strange place when I could feel my magic running through my veins.

For a minute, I wondered what to do? Should I stay here and wait for the others to find me? Should I go after my friends? Should I do it quietly, or shout for them?

I decided to walk the way I thought I had come and called

for them. If Muma Padurii showed up, I would then come up with a new plan.

A long time passed while I walked and shouted my friends' names, and with each passing minute, the panic grew in my chest. I was lost. Only Artan had a map of the forest. I could tell where north and south were if I looked at the sky, but it was getting late and I didn't know how to read the stars. The idea of being alone in this forest at night scared the crap out of me. I had to find my friends.

Whispers came from my right.

"Artan?" I asked, turning that way.

Then whispers came from my left.

"Guys?" I turned to my left.

The whispers continued, circling me, as if they were taunting me.

A chill ran down my spine and I ran, screaming my friends' names.

"Theron!" I shouted again. "Ellie!"

"Mirella!" I heard back, a faint call, but I heard it.

"Where are you?" I asked, trying to be louder.

"Here!"

I ran toward the voice. In the distance, Ellie appeared from the trees, running toward me. We crashed into each other, hugging tight.

"I'm so glad to see you," I said.

"Me too!" She squeezed me some more. "I thought that crazy creature had taken you and—" She pulled back, her lips a thin line. "I don't want to think about it."

"We need to find the others."

"I know."

I glanced around. The forest looked the same everywhere I turned. Tall, thick trees, exposed roots, many bushes and vines, and a mix of dirt ground and fallen leaves. "Any idea where they went?"

"I have no idea where we are. How am I supposed to know where they could be?"

"Touché." I sighed. "I guess we better keep searching and hope we find them soon."

I really hoped we found them soon. Muma Padurii could not be the only thing lurking in this forest, and if something else attacked us, we might not be so lucky. I could barely control my magic, and I had no fighting skills. We needed Artan and Theron.

Hands linked, Ellie and I walked through the forest. The thought that we could be walking in a circle and would have no idea hit me like a truck, but instead of stopping and wallowing in pity, I decided to keep moving. At least I felt less useless like that.

The forest sounds—snapping of twigs, the sounds of squirrels getting ready for winter, of the leafless branches moving in the breeze, and the damn whispers—sent chills up my spine. I was also sure I spotted oddly shaped shadows among the trees and behind bushes.

I opted for talking over it all.

"So, are you going to tell me why you insisted on coming with us?" I asked.

Ellie glanced at me, her brows furrowed. "I guess ... I don't know. I mean ..."

"Just say it."

"Maybe I was jealous."

I stopped dead in my tracks. "What? Of what?"

She pulled her hand away. "Of you."

My eyes widened. "But ... why?"

She averted her eyes. "You are this special person, twice

over. I mean, you're a tzigane, which is already pretty special, and then you're someone special even to them. You're living a fairy tale, a great adventure, while I am trapped in my crappy routine, going from the dorm to my classes and back."

"Special? Great adventure? Crappy routine? Ellie, you know I would switch places with you in the blink of an eye." What the hell was she talking about? She had been kidnapped by alchemists because of me and the fact that I was a Tzigane. She should hate me. And yet, she was jealous?

"I know, and that didn't make sense at first. Why would you want to run away and give up your powers and this amazing life the tziganes are offering you?"

I just stared at her. Was she for real? "But—"

"I know, I get it," she interrupted me. "After going to Lovell with you and seeing your mother and hearing first-hand about the other tziganes, I get it. I practically felt the pressure on your shoulders and for the first time in a couple of weeks … I didn't want to be you."

"Oh, Ellie …"

"But when you mentioned a mission, a little tiny spark started in my chest." She pressed her hand over her heart. "I thought this was my chance at having an adventure too. I know the circumstances are dire, and I shouldn't get excited about it, but I am." She shrugged. "Well, I was until that crazy creature attacked us and I realized this is real life, not a fairy tale. In fairy tales, no matter the hardships and obstacles, there's always a happy ending. In real life, that might not be the case." She paused. "I'm sorry."

"I don't know if I should punch you or hug you right now."

"Maybe both? Not that I'm fond of punching, but I think I do kinda deserved it."

I shook my head once and took her hands on mine. "Please, don't feel jealous of me ever again. The heart maiden thing might sound cool in theory, but so far it has been pretty rough, and I bet it'll only get worse."

"I know … I know that now. I'm sorry."

I pulled her to me and wrapped my arms around her. "It's okay. I'm actually glad you're here with me right now. Better being lost with my best friend than alone."

She chuckled. "Yeah, though it sucks for the best friend, who could have been safe and sound in her dorm right now."

I pulled away and slapped her shoulder. "You suck …"

"I know," she said, serious again. "I'm really sorry."

"Stop apologizing. Just promise me you'll never feel jealous or jump headfirst into anything because it looks special or fun. I assure you, it never is."

A small smile tugged at her lips. "I promise."

A couple of twigs snapped somewhere to our side and both of us turned that way.

Felix appeared from behind the trees.

"There you are," Theron said, appearing beside the lion.

Artan was right behind him. "Are you two okay?"

"I think so," I said. Theron walked over a thick root and winced. His hand was pressed to the side of his stomach. "What happened?"

"Those damn vines," Theron said, his voice a little weak. "It's just a little scratch. I'll be fine."

They halted by our side.

"What do we do now?" I asked, running my hand over Felix's big head.

Artan had the map in his hand. "If Muma Padurii doesn't show up, I say we keep moving until the sun sets. Then we set up camp."

Set up camp in this forest? Where Muma Padurii lurked and ruled? I didn't like that, but it seemed we had no other choice.

"What he said," Theron agreed.

Without another word, Artan led the way and we followed.

"One of you two want to explain to me what Muma Padurii is exactly?" I asked, hoping Artan or Theron knew the answer.

"She's a forest protector," Theron said.

Right, Artan had said as much, but I wanted to know more. "She simply attacks whoever enters the forest?"

"Not exactly," Artan said. "She probably thought we came to do some harm, but either way, Muma Padurii has a twisted sense of humor."

Interesting. Creepy. "Does every forest have a Muma Padurii or is there only one? How does that work?"

"Nobody knows," Theron said. "Some people believe it's the same Muma Padurii protecting all the forests in the entire world."

"And some people believe there are several," Artan added. "Either way, it's magic. If it's only one or more, she or they are pure forest magic."

I shuddered. "I just hope we don't meet her again."

"Me too," Ellie said.

It only took another hour for the sun to set. We found a secluded area beside a large boulder and surrounded by trees. Theron put down his backpack and pulled out a thin blanket from it. Ellie helped him spread it over the dirty ground, then he sat down with his back resting against the boulder. Even though they started arguing again, Ellie helped Theron with his scratch—it was worse than he had made it sound, but not too bad. The blood was already caked over and some healing paste and bandages would work great.

A couple of feet behind us, Felix lay down on the ground and rested his big head on his front paws, as if he was ready to crash. Meanwhile, Artan gathered some firewood, put it all in a little mound in the middle of our camp, surrounded it with stones, and asked me to light a fire.

I placed my hand over the firewood and called on my power.

"Just ... relax," Artan said from beside me, his voice gentle. "The fire is part of you; just let it come."

I glanced at him, at his intense amber eyes, at the mysterious shine in them. The fire inside me answered and rushed to my hand. The wood creaked under my palm as the fire spread.

One corner of his lips curled up. "Not bad."

I snorted, pulling my hand away. "Terrible, you mean?"

I leaned into the fire, appreciating its warmth. Artan sat down beside me. "No, not terrible. Not in the least. You're doing great. And you gotta keep in mind you're still learning, so it'll take time."

"We don't have time."

The fire crackled. Its light played with the shadows and sharp angles of Artan's handsome face, making him even seem more mysterious, more enticing.

"I'm confident in you."

I narrowed my eyes at him. "What changed?"

"What do you mean?"

"Until a couple of days ago, you were mean to me, drilling me about fighting and sparring, and yelling at me when I defied the council, or decided to go to class instead of training. You've criticized every choice I've made, every word I've uttered." I paused. "What changed?"

He stared at me with those two molten embers for a minute before answering, "Everything changed."

I waited, thinking he would say more, explain what he meant, but instead, he stood.

"What happened?" I asked.

He grabbed his backpack. "We should eat something, then rest."

I was about to get up and make him explain to me what the hell he meant, but Ellie appeared between us.

"Good idea. I'm hungry and I'm beat," she said.

Artan opened a small picnic cloth between the four of us, and we all placed the little food we had brought on it—bread, cheese, dried meat, fruit, and slices of cake. Since we couldn't heat or cook anything out here, our food choice had to be simple.

In no time, we all ate and opened our sleeping bags.

"I'll take the first watch," Artan said. He and Theron organized a weird night schedule, alternating between both of them. When I offered to take a couple of hours, they cut me off, saying I should rest. "We've got this."

With Felix right beside me, I slipped inside my sleeping bag and closed my eyes, trying to sleep. With the night filled with odd forest noises, and knowing Muma Padurii was somewhere out there, knowing she could attack us while we were sleeping, I doubted I would get any rest.

Artan folded a blanket in front of the fire and sat down on it, his sword right beside him. He glanced at me. "Good night."

"Good night," I said. Then I forced my eyes closed.

Only a minute seemed to have passed before whispers

reached my ears. I groaned and turned in my sleeping bag, trying not to snap at whoever was talking while I tried to sleep.

A breeze blew past, making the whispers sound louder.

I pushed up on my elbows. "What the hell? Can't you guys be quiet?" I looked to the side and saw Ellie's sleeping bag empty. I sat up with a start. "Ellie?"

There, several feet in front of me, Ellie walked off into the woods.

15

"Ellie!" I called her, but she didn't stop. I glanced at Artan, who was seated by the fire, staring straight ahead. "Artan, did she say something to you?" He didn't answer me. "Hey, I'm talking to you."

Again, there was only silence.

Then I heard it. The whispers. They were the same from before, from when I was alone in the forest, looking for my friends. But this time, they were louder. Hushed words in a language I didn't understand.

"Do you hear that?" I asked.

Artan didn't say anything. He also didn't move. He didn't even blink.

A chill ran down my spine.

I yelped when Theron suddenly sat up and, like a mummy, rose to his feet, and walked toward the forest too.

"Theron, stop," I called, standing up. I rushed to him. "Don't listen to it. To them. To whatever this is." I grabbed his arm and tried holding him back, but he simply kept walking, dragging me along.

I let go of him and faced Artan, who was still seated and staring off. I snapped my fingers in front of his face. He didn't blink.

Desperation bloomed in my chest. By Saint Sara-la-Kali, what was I going to do?

The whispers intensified, the shadows around the camp grew, and the bonfire seemed to be half the size it was a minute ago.

Artan shot to his feet, startling me, and like Ellie and Theron, he started marching toward the forest like a robot.

"Please, stop," I called, my voice breaking.

Next, Felix rose from his corner.

"The shadows aren't calling you, right?"

I reached into his mind—and encountered a wall of steel. Felix's mind wasn't his and I couldn't access it. Like the others, Felix ignored me and strolled into the forest.

I grabbed a small branch from the bonfire, hoping it was enough of a light, and ran after them. I lifted the branch high, but I couldn't see more than a few feet around me. I could hear them though. All of them—Ellie, Theron, Artan, Felix, and the shadows.

Something brushed against my back, and yelping, I recoiled. I spun on my heels, but there was nothing behind me. Or in front of me. The whispers became like hissed chants—fast muttered words.

Almost like ... a spell?

Something like a hand brushed against my knee and I jumped, screaming. My heart lodged in my throat and my hands trembled. The shine from the branch in my hand flickered with my rapid movements, making the shadows that seemed to move in the dark look like monsters.

I closed my eyes.

This can't be real. This can't be real.

"This can't be real," I said, opening my eyes.

Whatever this was, it lived in the shadows. If I could only make the shadow disappear ...

A gasp rippled through my throat as an idea came into my mind.

I knelt down and touched the tip of the branch on the ground. I channeled my magic. My hand grew hot and red. The branch became like coal and fire shot out of its tip, trailing ahead like a serpent. On and on it went, creating a thin trail of fire and illuminating the forest.

Then I saw them. Felix about ten feet to my left, Artan about eight feet to my right, and Theron and Ellie fifteen feet ahead of me.

The branch in my hand snapped and fire enclosed my hand. I stood and raised my hand high. The flame in my hand along with the serpent of fire were brighter than sunlight.

The shadows retreated. The whispers stopped.

Felix let out a loud roar.

Artan blinked and stared at me. "What happened?"

Theron and Ellie jumped over my fire serpent and rushed to us.

I inhaled deeply, extinguishing the serpent, but keeping the flame in my hand strong and bright. "You wouldn't believe me."

We made our way back to the camp and I told them what had happened.

"That's crazy," Theron said, rolling his sleeping bag.

Ellie clicked her tongue. "Everything about you guys is crazy."

Theron glanced at her. "What do you mean?"

"Well, if I didn't know what you guys can do, if I hadn't seen it with my own eyes, I would certainly say you're all crazy. Like nut-house crazy."

"Thanks," Theron grumbled.

I rolled up my sleeping bag. "What now?"

Artan folded his blanket and put it inside his backpack. "The sun will be up in thirty minutes or so. I say we break camp and get moving. The sooner we find Cianna, the better."

"But what about the shadows?" I asked, not too eager to go out there until the sun was up. And even then, the dangers of the forest were proving too many.

He offered me that half smile of his. "Well, you conjure fire again and keep them back with it. By the way, what you did was great. You're already improving."

"I don't think that's improving. That's just acting when I'm desperate."

"If that's what it takes …"

I frowned. "What does that mean? You're not thinking of putting me in danger during training, are you? I won't play along if you are."

He let out a small chuckle. "We can talk about that later."

Felix kept marching around the camp while we rolled our bags and put away our food, as if patrolling the perimeter and making sure we were safe. But hadn't he just walked away like a lion-zombie? He had been easily thwarted. What if that happened again?

"Let's go," Theron said, pulling me out from the dark depths of my crazy mind.

The five of us marched away, into the forest, into the unknown, into danger.

A few minutes later, Felix started snarling.

"What is it, boy?" I asked, already wary.

He conjured an image in my mind.

"We're being followed," Artan whispered, taking the words out of my mouth.

He slowed down and pretended to fuss with my backpack.

Theron came up on my other side, keeping Ellie in front of us.

Fast like a snake, Artan spun around and shot his hand through a tall bush. He pulled out an old woman, his hand wrapped around her neck.

She stared at us with wide eyes. "You got me."

16

ARTAN PUSHED THE OLD LADY AGAINST A TREE TRUNK AND gritted his teeth. "Who are you?"

The old woman stared at him, her dark green eyes round. "I'm ... I'm ..."

I placed my hand on Artan's arm. "Let her go, Artan. You're hurting her."

"She could be Muma Padurii playing with us again."

"Muma Padurii?" the old woman gasped. "That old hag played with you?"

"She attacked us, actually," I said. I tugged on Artan's arm.

"Oh, that's not good," the old lady said, her voice kind. "She has a temper, that old hag."

Artan finally stepped back, letting go of the poor old lady. "You know her?"

The old lady ran a hand over her long, messy gray braid, and her brown skirt. "I live here, don't I? I often see her around. Or, actually, she comes to check on me. I guess she doesn't trust me a hundred percent, even though I've been living here for many years."

"Living here?" I mumbled.

"What were you doing?" Theron asked. "Why were you following us?"

"I was gathering herbs for my salves." She pointed to the wicker basket on the ground a few feet to the side. "I heard you marching by. It's rare to see humans or tziganes around this area. I guess I wanted to make sure you were friendly before I said hello."

"So, you're a tzigane?" Ellie asked.

"Oh, yes." The old woman straightened her back. "I'm Cianna. Nice to meet you."

"Cianna!" I practically screamed.

The old woman flinched, startled. "Yes?"

"We're here for you," I said.

She looked at me like I was crazy. "What?"

Then, I told her that I was the heart maiden, that I felt the flower, but couldn't follow it, that the enclaves have been without elixir from the flower for a long time, and now tziganes were getting sick and soon would die if I didn't find the flower.

"My mother fell sick yesterday," I said, the words getting stuck on my throat.

Theron put a hand over my shoulder. "Yes, Marisa tried to be strong for Mirella, but it was too much for her."

The old woman's eyes bugged and she opened her mouth. "And h-how did you find out about me?"

"My mother said to come find you. She said you should have some spare elixir from the heart flower we could borrow from you."

"S-she did?"

"Yes," I said, tilting my head. "How do you know her?"

The woman waved me off. "That's not important. What is important is that we go to my cabin and get the elixir."

My heart skipped two, three beats. "So you have it?"

Cianna's lips became a thin line. "I do, but I'm afraid it won't be enough for your entire enclave."

"Any bit helps," I said, too eager to put my hands on the elixir. I would worry about it not being enough later.

"Then we have no time to waste. Let's go." Energized, Cianna marched ahead, beckoning us to follow her.

Artan shot me a wary look, but I dismissed him. I wouldn't let his worries and bad mood burst my bubble. We were almost there! We would succeed!

A few minutes walking up the mountain, our group fell into a formation. Cianna and me in front, Artan and Felix a few feet behind us, and Theron and Ellie in the back.

The only sound was the crunch of leaves under our boots, the ruffling of thin branches in the wind, and the occasional chirp of a bird or a squeak from a squirrel. It was peaceful. Then, curiosity swelled in me and I couldn't hold the questions any longer.

"So," I started, glancing to Cianna. "What's your story?"

She narrowed her eyes at me. "What do you mean?"

"Since learning I'm a tzigane, I was told over and over that tziganes are stronger together. That's why they live in enclaves and do everything together. And yet, you're living in the mountains alone. May I ask why?"

She tsked. "People have different personalities, even tziganes. I was never one for the crowd and doing everything as one. I prefer the peace and quiet."

She was hiding something, but I didn't want to pry. Perhaps it was too painful and she didn't want to remember it.

Instead, I asked a question I thought wouldn't hurt as much. "How long have you been living here?"

"For about eighteen years, I think."

For eighteen years, she had been here alone. I understood the need for peace and quiet, but I couldn't imagine cutting out of civilization for eighteen years.

"How do you know my mother?"

She smiled at me. "Aren't we curious?"

My cheeks flamed. "Sorry. It's just ... she never mentioned you, and when I told the council I wanted to find you, Darcy went berserk."

Cianna's smile fell. "Ugh, Darcy. That's one old hag I can't stomach." I chuckled. Cianna glanced at me. "What?"

"Old hag," I said in a low voice. "That's what I call her. Just don't let Artan hear you. He's her grandson. He knows she's difficult, but I'm not sure he would take kindly to someone calling her an old hag in front of him."

Cianna snorted. "Duly noted."

The fact that she didn't answer any of my questions didn't escape me, but I didn't push. Her story wasn't important as long as she had the elixir. Nothing else mattered. Not right now.

The mountainside became steeper, and thirty minutes later, I was panting and my legs hurt.

"How much longer?" Ellie asked from the back, echoing the question in my mind.

"Just a few more minutes," Cianna said, charging ahead.

She zigzagged through a patch of thick, close trees, but at least the ground wasn't as steep here. The trees opened to a large landing and a small wooden cabin resting at the edge of a cliff. A small Romani vurdon sat beside it, surrounded by colorful flowers—at this time of the year, I guessed she worked some of her magic to keep them alive.

I sighed in relief. We made it. We had found Cianna, and now she would give me the elixir and we would be on our way. By tomorrow, I would give the elixir to everyone in the enclave. Everyone would be cured, including my mother, and I would have more time to worry about following the flower's call.

My relief was short-lived as I looked up. "Oh no."

"Hello again," Muma Padurii said, seated atop of the cabin's roof.

17

ARTAN WAS IN FRONT OF ME IN A FLASH, HIS SWORD IN HAND. Joining him, Felix stepped forward and growled at the mad forest protector.

"What do you want?" Theron asked, coming to stand by my side. His hand was on the hilt of his sword.

Muma Padurii let out a witch-like laugh. "Is that how you say hello to a friend?"

"Whose friend?" I glanced to Cianna. "Don't tell me she's your friend."

Cianna shook her head, her eyes wide. "No, no. Muma doesn't have friends. We mostly tolerate each other. She doesn't bother me as long as I don't hurt her forest."

"That's right," Muma said, standing up. "So far, you've been doing a good job."

"What do you want?" Theron asked again, his voice louder.

Muma tilted her head at him. "I wanted to know how it was. The shadows and the trance. Did you like my game?"

My mouth fell open. "That was you?"

"Yes, and it was fun. You should sleep outside tonight and we can play again."

Rage swept through me. This woman was making me crazy. "If you're not here to tell me where the damn heart flower is, then you should leave," I said, trying to sound sure and confident, though my hands shook with anger and frustration.

Cianna waved her arm toward Muma. "Go away, Muma."

Muma put her tree-like hand over her chest and gasped. "I feel like I'm not wanted here."

"You think?" Ellie asked, her voice trembling. She too was trying to be brave, and I admired her for that.

"But we were having so much fun, weren't we?" She sounded crazy. Like she was high or something. "We're gonna have more fun now."

What did she mean?

She opened her arms to the sky and loud roars filled the air.

The hair on my neck stood on end.

At first, the three figures looked like birds coming at us, but their shape grew and grew and grew. I gasped when they finally were close enough and I could see them.

Dragons. Big, winged, drag—

"Wyverns," Cianna said from behind me.

"W-what?"

Theron pulled out his sword. "Shit."

We retreated several steps when the three creatures sat on the roof of the cabin. Their huge talons sank into the logs as if they were made of rubber, and they turned their big, dragon-like heads toward us. Their brown, slick skin gleamed in the sun, and their red eyes seemed evil.

I thought I had been scared when I had to face revenants.

Twice. But that was only because I had no idea there could be bigger, scarier, monstrous creatures than them.

A lump of fear choked me.

"T-they sure do look like dragons," I muttered, clutching Artan's arm.

"Wyverns are smaller and they have only two legs," Artan said.

"Smaller?" To me they seemed huge. Their talons were probably the size of my arms. Then, it sank in. "Wait, dragons are real?"

Theron glanced at me, his eyes narrowed. "There's a freaking wyvern in front of you. Why would you doubt dragons?"

"Shush," Cianna said, her eyes on the three animals nesting on her home. "They are watching us. Don't make any sudden moves or they will attack."

"Won't they attack anyway?" Artan asked.

"Probably," Cianna confessed.

"Hey, w-where's Muma?" Ellie asked, hiding behind Theron.

We all glanced to the roof, to the Wyverns, to the cabin, to the sides.

Muma Padurii was nowhere to be seen.

"I hate her," Artan hissed under his breath.

"You're not the only one," Theron said.

"What now?" I asked, my gaze flicking from one beast to another.

They opened and closed their wings and snapped their razor-sharp teeth, making me jump with each clinking sound. Their red eyes were fixed at us, but other than that, they didn't move.

I swallowed.

"They won't leave until we make them leave," Cianna said.

"You mean ..."

She looked at me, her green eyes grave. "We have to fight them."

Shit. "And how do you fight a wyvern?"

"Well ..." Cianna looked out and gasped. "Watch out."

One of the wyverns jumped up, and soared toward us.

Instinctively, we ducked and jumped out of the way. Artan held my wrist and pulled me with him, while Theron did the same with Ellie, but away from us. And Felix and Cianna ended on the other side of the beast, closer to the cabin.

Felix growled at the wyvern, drawing its attention. The creature turned, whipping its long, spiked tail. Holding me tight, Artan used his air power to blast us even farther from the group—and away from the tail that would have smacked us in the stomach and sent us flying into the trees.

A spray of water blasted the wyvern and it shrieked.

"What ..."

Another wave of water washed over the beast. It screamed, flapped its big wings, snapped its teeth, and drank water as a shower rained down on it. In awe, I stared as the creature took flight and landed back on the roof, shaking everything.

That was when I saw Cianna with her palms up and a dancing ball of water in front of her. She waved her hand and a snake of water peeked out from a wooden barrel beside the porch. She threw her arm toward the beasts and the water followed, squirting the wyverns.

She could control water. That was actually pretty cool.

But the water was angering the creatures. The first wyvern snapped its sharp teeth at the other two, who snapped back, as if they were arguing. Then, with a low swoop, the two other wyverns came for us.

Felix and Cianna dealt with one, while Theron and Artan advanced on the second one. The guys used air to blast it back and swords to hurt it.

Holding hands, Ellie and I watched the commotion. Ellie was shaking, and I guess I was too. But I wanted to do more than cower and hope my friends saved the day. I wanted to help.

Taking a deep breath, I let go of Ellie's hand and channeled my magic. I felt as the fire awakened and spread through my veins. I smiled at its power, its comfortable warmth.

I raised my hand, ready to shoot the wyverns, but Artan and Theron kept dancing in front of me, blocking the beast. I could try and hit the wyvern, but I would risk hitting one of the guys too. I took two steps to the side and watched the wyvern with Cianna and Felix—the situation there wasn't much better. Cianna kept blasting the creature with water, while Felix scratched his long claws at the beast's limbs. Like Artan and Theron, Cianna and Felix didn't stop moving side to side, up and down, front and back. There was no clear shot for me.

My shoulders sagged and I lowered my arms.

The third wyvern bellowed and stomped on the roof, shaking the small cabin. Then its eyes locked on mine. It let out a loud screech and jumped.

Right in front of me.

I clambered back, pulling Ellie with me. But in her shock, Ellie tripped and the beast jumped over her, pinning her to the ground. Ellie cried and I panicked. The creature snapped its teeth inches from Ellie's face.

Something broke inside me, like a dam, but instead of water, it was made entirely of fire.

I threw my hands up, and yelling, I let it out.

Fire burst from my hands, shooting toward the wyvern. My fire exploded on its skin, and the creature shrieked, retreating. Snapping its teeth toward me, the creature fought the fire, but it was visibly singeing its skin. The wyvern was weakening. I focused and sent another wave of power through my veins, into my fire.

The wyvern roared, then opened its mighty wings. They flapped twice, before the creature pushed up and flew away.

Without wasting time, I turned to the wyvern closest to me. Cianna and Felix retreated as I threw fire at the creature. Like the first one, the monster cried and tried to resist the fire, but in the end, it flew away.

Then, I went for the third one. It had its back to me, and when my fire licked its skin, the wyvern let out a shriek and jumped back. It tried advancing three times, but it always ended up retreating and swinging its body from side to side, moving its tail, and slamming the porch of Cianna's cabin.

"Leave already!" I screamed, pushing more force, more magic into the fire.

Finally, the wyvern pushed the ground with its legs and flew away.

Letting out a long breath, I released my magic and lowered my arms. It was like a weight sat on my shoulders and I was dragged down. Black dots swimming in my vision, I fell on my knees.

"Mirella!" Artan called, rushing to me. Strong arms cradled me, and I leaned back against his hard chest. "I've got you."

Holding Ellie's arm, Theron stopped in front of me. "What happened? Are you okay?"

Cianna crouched down beside me. She took my arm and checked my pulse. "She's drained, but she'll be all right." She beckoned us into the cabin. "Let's bring her inside. I should have some healing elixir with my supplies."

Artan passed his arms under my arms and knees and pulled me up.

"I ... I can walk," I whispered, still feeling weak.

"I'm not taking any chances," he said, his voice harsh.

Felix circled us as we walked up the porch steps until Cianna stopped by the door and looked at him. "Sorry, but no animals inside my house." She opened the door and went inside.

At once, Felix plopped down on the porch, looking out at the trees in the distance, as if he was our assigned guard.

Are you okay? I asked him.

An image of me falling to the ground filled my mind. He was worried about me.

I'll be fine, I assured him.

He didn't seem to believe me, or maybe he didn't care.

I was gonna tell him something else to make him feel better about it, but then we were inside the cabin and all I could do was gawk.

Gently, Artan dropped me on a couch while he too stared at the place.

Cianna's cabin was cute and small with rustic furniture and lots of colorful cushions and rugs and curtains. Beads hung from the doorways and colorful lanterns from the ceiling.

However, it was all a mess.

There were holes in the roof, pieces of log on the floor,

wood dust on the furniture, and lots of things had been knocked over—lamps, portraits, mirrors, and shelves. Shelves full of books and vials and elixirs.

"What happened here?" Ellie asked, looking around.

Frowning, Cianna knelt beside the fallen shelf. "The wyverns. They shook the cabin when they sat on it." A tightness and sadness filled her voice.

I shot up and dizziness spun my head. I put a hand on Artan's arm to steady myself. "Don't tell me …"

Among the many broken vials on the ground, Cianna picked a few pieces of glass and lifted them. "Here was the elixir."

My heart sank and my knees wobbled again. Artan's grip tightened around my hand.

No, this couldn't be true. There had to be more. Somewhere. Anywhere.

"No," Theron muttered, shaking his head. "No, no. We didn't come all this way to have it broken minutes before we could get it."

"I'm sorry," Cianna said. Careful with the broken glass, she rummaged through the mess and pulled a half broken vial. There was a little blue liquid at the bottom. "This is the healing elixir. I can drain it to make sure it's free of any glass and then you should drink some." With automatic movements, she shot to her feet and went to the small kitchen in the corner.

I sank down on the couch and Artan sat beside me.

He squeezed my hand again. "What now?"

"I don't know," I muttered.

I was lost. I was empty.

What was I going to do now? All our hopes had been thrown on this woman and her spare elixir. We had ventured out on a mission, my first mission, to come here, and for what? To have it all snatched from our hands. It felt like I was trying to hold on to water with my bare hands.

By Saint Sara-la-Kali, what was I going to do? The entire enclave depended on me. My mother's life depended on me.

Tears brimmed in my eyes, and not wanting to cry in front of Artan or anyone else, I blinked.

"Here." Cianna came back with a tray and several non-matching teacups. She set the tray on a splintered table in front of the couch. She pointed to a cup. "This one is yours, Mirella. It has the healing elixir."

"Thank you," Theron said.

I was glad he spoke up, because I wasn't sure I could ever say anything again.

With tears in her eyes, Cianna stared at me. "I'm sorry. I'm really sorry. I didn't have a lot of the heart elixir, but I was going to give you all I had." She glanced to the overturned shelf and sniffed. "Now it's all gone."

Artan shot to his feet. "We can help you clean up." He nudged Theron.

"Right," Theron said, sounding not too enthusiastic about the prospect. He glanced up. "We can start by patching the roof."

"Good idea," Artan said. "Then while outside, we should see what else was damaged."

Cianna guided them outside, saying something about having some tools on the vurdon.

Ellie sat down beside me. She reached to the tray and

picked up my teacup. "Drink this." I stared at the cup. "Please." She practically shoved it into my hand, so I took it.

Defeated, I sipped from the tea. It was sweet and warm, but laced with a bitter taste. The healing elixir. I scrunched my nose. "This is horrible."

"Drink more," Ellie insisted. "You'll feel better after."

Would I feel better? Physically maybe, but not emotionally. This elixir wouldn't mend the broken vials and recover the spilled elixirs.

Holding my breath, I downed the tea. Then shuddered as the bitter taste filled my mouth. "Ugh."

At least, I could feel it already working, already giving me a boost of energy.

"Here, have mine." Ellie handed me another teacup. Shaking my head, I pushed it aside. I didn't mind the bitter taste. It was actually good, because it felt like some kind of punishment, a small one, for having failed. Once again, I had failed. "I'm sorry."

I nodded, not sure what to say. What could I say? The elixir and the chance to save my mother and all the other tziganes was gone.

Tears filled my eyes and I wiped them off. Needing something to occupy my mind and soul before I broke down, I shot to my feet. "Let's clean up in here," I said.

I felt Ellie frozen on the spot, watching me as if I had grown an extra head, while I looked around the kitchen, searching for a broom and some rags. After grabbing rags from a drawer and finding the broom on a small closet outside the kitchen, I went to the fallen shelf.

Liquids of all colors, and glasses of all sizes and shapes mixed under the broken wood. Slowly, I grasped the wood and pulled the shelf up.

"I'll help you," Ellie said, snapping out of her trance. She rushed to me and helped me pull the shelf up and rest it against the wall. It was broken and bent. Repairing wouldn't be enough. It would need to be replaced.

I stared at the wasted elixirs on the floor, my heart hurting again.

And these were all going to the trash. No repairing and no replacing for them.

For the next hour, we cleaned and helped in silence—other than the hammering outside, coming from the roof repairs.

I wondered though, what would we do now? Finish helping Cianna, then go home? But as much as I raked my mind, I couldn't see any other options.

I was sweeping the kitchen when Cianna entered the cabin.

"Oh, dear, you don't need to do that," she said, waving me off.

My grip around the broom tightened. "I want to."

She pursed her lips, but then gave me her back and filled two glasses with water. "The sun will be setting soon. I have only two bedrooms, but enough spare comforters and pillows. You and your friends should spend the night here." I opened my mouth to protest, but she continued, "I assure you it's better than walking down the mountain and having to sleep in the forest with Muma Padurii out there."

Damn, she was right. I would rather spend the night here, even if I had to sleep on the floor, than risk spending more time at Muma's mercy.

"I'll talk to my friends," I said. I knew Artan and Theron would be wary of Cianna's invite—it was the warrior in them —but they too would see it was the better option.

"Good." She offered me a tight smile. "Then let me know so I can fix us something for supper and make the beds." Gripping the glasses, she turned and started walking away.

I was watching her, wondering once more why she lived so far from others, so deep in the mountains, what had driven her here, and how did she have spare heart elixir, when it hit me.

The sweet scent of flowers filled my nostrils, and scorching warmth filled my chest, making me gasp. It pulsed and squeezed, making me dizzy.

I could see it.

The heart flower.

A beautiful meadow and the flower sprouting from among low bushes. Alone, beautiful, radiant.

Only a few steps from me. I stretched my hand to get it …

"Mirella!"

I blinked. "W-what?" Confused, I glanced around. I was leaning over the kitchen counter, my hand raised in front of me. I lowered it, but the feeling, the warmth was still there, making it hard to breathe.

"What's happening?" Cianna asked. She was standing right in front of me, the two glasses of water resting on the counter to her side. She knotted her brows. "What was that?"

Ellie, who had been tidying the living room, rushed to our side. "It's the call, right? The heart flower's call?"

Resting my hand over my heated heart, I nodded. "Y-yes."

"Can you follow it?" she asked, hope laced in her words.

I closed my eyes and tried to see it, to follow it. To conjure a path to that meadow.

But nothing happened. Even when I pictured the meadow now, it didn't feel as real and vivid as it had a few moments ago.

"I can't," I admitted, feeling like a failure again.

"I still don't understand how you can't follow the flower," Cianna said.

I looked down at my feet, embarrassed. Sick. Hurt. "Me neither."

Cianna took a deep inhale, a loud, raspy thing that made me look at her. She was staring at me. "There's a place here in the mountains, a little over half a day hike, which is supposed to be magical." She furrowed her brows. "I know it's magical; I've been there once. Anyway, I think … I think that if you try to follow the heart flower's call from there, it might work."

"Wait, what? Why would it work?"

"I'm not sure it'll work," she said quickly. "But that place is powerful and it always amplifies my magic. I bet it can amplify the call and your powers, and maybe you'll be able to follow it."

I staggered over two words of her sentence. Amplify—I could barely control my magic as it was. If we amplified it, only Saint Sara-la-Kali could tell the terrible things that might happen.

And maybe—maybe I would be able to follow it. There was no way to know for sure.

"I don't know," I mumbled.

"You should at least try," Cianna insisted. "The place is called Hollow's Bane and I've been there before."

I frowned. Hollow's Bane. My mother had mentioned this place when telling me about Cianna. Still, it felt too far-fetched, too easy, too convenient.

"If you really believe that, then we should go now," Ellie said. "Half a day's hike. Maybe we can get there before midnight."

"I don't think—"

The door burst open and Theron marched in, a hand over his stomach. "I need help," he said.

"What—?" Ellie gasped upon seeing the blood seeping from underneath his hand. "Your wound."

"Yeah." He grimaced. "I think that with the hard work outside, it opened."

Ellie ushered Theron to a chair in the kitchen.

"I'll get my first aid kit," Cianna said. "And a healing salve, if I still have one." She turned to me. "Think about it, then let me know. But my opinion, dear. At this point, you have nothing to lose by trying."

Ellie fussed over Theron and Cianna soon was back with a shoebox filled with gauze and other things. It seemed he was well served, so I grabbed one of the glasses filled with water from the counter and went outside.

Some pillars from the porch were still broken and bent, but new support beams were in place. The *bang bang* of the hammer echoed through the clearing.

"Artan," I called, hoping I didn't need to yell for him to hear me. "I brought water."

The hammering stopped. With a swoosh of air, Artan jumped off the roof and gracefully landed in front of me.

His amber hair was damp and glued to his handsome face. He had taken off the vest of his warrior uniform and several buttons of his shirt were undone. Underneath, his golden skin glistened with sweat. The sleeves were folded to his elbows, and when he raised his arm and swept the sweat off his face, the muscles in his fore and upper arms corded.

Swallowing hard, I averted my eyes and stretched the glass to him.

"Thank you," he said, taking the glass from me.

I waited a few seconds and said, "I just felt the call of the flower again. Stronger this time."

"And?"

I returned my eyes to him. "I still can't follow it. But Cianna said there's a magical place half a day hike from here. She said that place can amplify magic. She thinks it will amplify my power and the flower's call."

He frowned. "So we're to blindly follow her to an unknown place farther into the mountains."

I knew he wouldn't like it.

"You have any other idea? Besides, we're in the middle of nowhere in a cabin with her. If she wants to do us harm, she doesn't need to take us anywhere."

He shook his head once. "I don't like this."

"I don't like anything that is happening, and yet I can't change it." I looked down at my hands. "I'm a failure, and I can't change it."

Artan set down his empty glass and reached for my hands. "Mirella, you're not a failure. Far from that."

His amber eyes danced with the sunset light. So entrancing. "What should we do?"

"If you think we should go with her to this place, then we will." He squeezed my hands.

"Even if you don't like it."

One corner of his lips curled up. "Even if I don't like it." Then his half-smile faded and the shine in his eyes intensified. "I'll follow you anywhere."

THE CABIN WAS ODDLY QUIET.

Granted, it wasn't even six in the morning. It was utterly dark out still, and everyone else was sleeping.

Everyone else but Artan and me.

Last night, after we decided to stay and finished cleaning up the cabin and repairing the roof as well as we could, Cianna made us an amazing meal—a creamy chicken casserole and baked potato seasoned to perfection. Later, we had more tea, warm showers, and Cianna showed us to our beds. She offered one of the bedrooms for me and Ellie and the other one to the guys.

"Where are you going to sleep?" I asked.

"The couch." She explained she was short and small and had slept on the couch many nights; it was okay.

But the guys intervened, saying they would take turns keeping watch during the night so there was no point in taking an entire bedroom for them. Cianna should sleep in her own bed, while Ellie and I took the guest bedroom. And the guys would take turns on the couch, too.

Cianna glanced to the couch, then to the two tall, strong guys in front of her. "That won't do."

Finally, they came to an agreement. She remembered having some bedrolls and extra comforters and pillows in the vurdon outside. Whoever wasn't up could sleep on the bedroll on the living room's floor. Not the best bed ever, but certainly better than the couch.

Careful not to make much noise and wake up Theron, who seemed to be sleeping like a stone in front of the couch, I made some tea, poured it in two mugs, and on tiptoes, I went outside.

I stopped at the edge of the porch and looked out at the darkness and the shadows that formed the trees. At first, I didn't see him, but he saw me from his privileged position.

Standing on the thick branch of a tall tree, Artan probably had a great view of the clearing, the cabin, and me.

Using his air powers, he did that jump-slash-floating thing that was more graceful every time I saw it. Like last evening, he landed right in front of me.

"Good morning," I said, handing him the second mug.

"Morning." He took the mug from me. "Shouldn't you still be sleeping?"

I sat on the porch steps and shrugged. "I barely slept." As usual. "What's the point? I keep tossing and turning and only get stressed about it. I prefer waking up and doing something."

A half-grin adorned his lips. "Like bringing tea to the warrior on duty."

I shrugged again. "I was making some for me, and I wasn't going to stay inside and risk making noise and waking up the others, so why not?"

He snorted. "Thanks." His expression softened and he sat beside me. "Want to talk about it?"

I looked at him. "About what?"

"Barely sleeping."

"There's not much to talk about."

He cocked an eyebrow. "How long has it been going on?"

I bit the inside of my cheek, thinking. "I'm not sure. Since this mess started, I guess."

"You mean the call of the flower and the sick tziganes."

I let out a hollow chuckle. "Yeah, no. Since I found out I was a tzigane and had alchemists chasing after me."

His brows furrowed. "That's not good. Have you talked to anyone about it?"

"I'm talking now," I said, forcing my voice to be mellow and cute.

With a soft grin, Artan shook his head. "You should have told me sooner."

"When? When you hated me and kept arguing with me and grilling me about everything I said or did? Yeah, as if I was gonna tell you anything then."

He glanced down at the steps. "I've never meant to be a jerk. I was just ... wary. I'm sorry about that." I sipped my tea, purposely ignoring him. I wouldn't say I accepted his apology now. That was long gone, I hoped, and he would never be that mean or callous to me again. "Hey," he said, his tone lower. Softer. "I mean it." He rested his hand on my arm. My heart stilled as I stared at his skin on mine. As I felt the warmth of his touch on me. "I'm sorry." I looked up at him and my breath caught. The first rays of the rising sun surged from behind the trees and made his amber eyes, so intent on mine, shine like liquid gold. "You mean a lot to me."

My heart skipped a beat.

In another time, in another year, I would be flirting with him. He would touch me or look at me like that, like he had done so many times in the last few weeks, and I would be all over that, even if he was being kind. I would try to convince him that he wanted to flirt back with me. That he wanted me. But that was before ... that was before Phillip. I knew, by Saint Sara-la-Kali, I knew Artan wasn't Phillip; he would never be. He wouldn't betray me like that. Artan had honor. Artan had merit. But ... it was hard. All of a sudden, walls had been erected around my heart, walls I didn't expect to have, and now I couldn't do much to bring them down.

Not yet.

Not alone.

Still staring at Artan, my heart clenched. Maybe with time, I would be okay with flirting again.

"I—"

"I mean," he started, pulling his hand away. "You mean a lot to all tziganes."

I gaped. So that was it? That was all I was? Just the heart maiden.

And here I thought, here I hoped, he finally saw me as more than the little fragile vase on a pedestal he had to watch over.

The sun rose some more, filling the sky with beautiful pink and orange hues.

I cleared my throat and stood. "I'll wake up the others so we can get going."

Without another glance back, I walked into the cabin.

NOT THIRTY MINUTES AFTER I WOKE EVERYONE UP, WE SET OUT. Since Cianna was the one who knew the mountains and the way to this magical place she told us about, she took the lead, charging ahead, full of energy for a woman who was probably in her late sixties, if not seventies.

Still upset with Artan, and not wanting to stand between Ellie and Theron, who were already arguing about stupid things, I fell into step with Cianna.

We remained silent for a long while, until finally she asked, "I can't imagine finding out you're the heart maiden so late in your life."

"H-how do you know I only found out recently?" I asked, on the defensive. "And I'm not old. I'm only twenty!"

She chuckled. "I didn't mean to imply you were old. Of course you aren't. But usually the heart maiden is found pretty early. Usually, before she's five years old.."

"How do you know that if there hasn't been a heart maiden in the last two hundred years?"

"Because that's what is written in our records and passed down through stories. If it's true ..." She shrugged. "No one really knows." She glanced at me. "As for your first question, Ellie told me about it while you showered last night. She seems like a good friend, even if she's a *gadjo*."

"I think I like her more because she *is* a *gadjo*."

The old woman chuckled again. "Defiant and stubborn. Just like your mother."

I almost tripped at the mention of my mother. One, I was worried sick wondering how she was doing, and two, Cianna still hadn't answered how she knew my mother.

"About that," I started. "You didn't ans—" I cut my words off when I felt Felix rushing to me. I braced myself and Felix bumped his big head into my legs hard, but not hard enough to make me fall. I glanced at him. "What is it, boy?"

Moving fast, he started circling me and projecting images in my mind. Another path. Tall trees opening to a meadow full of flowers. A stone cave jutting out from the side of the mountain. Many heart animals entering the meadow—lions, wolves, foxes, rabbits. All of them together, and simply strolling around the flowers, as if they were all friends, and not predators and prey.

Felix nudged his big nose on my thigh.

"What's happening?" Artan asked, coming to stand by my side.

"He's showing me something," I said as more images invaded my mind. The heart animals coming to stand in the middle of the meadow, forming a circle right in the center, as if they were looking at something. I tried spying over them, but I couldn't see past them, but it felt like ... I gasped. "I think he knows where it is."

Theron's eyes bulged. "What? The flower?"

"Yes," I said as eagerness, mostly coming from Felix, filled me. Felix wandered a few feet to our left and looked ahead. An image of the path through the trees flashed behind my eyes. "He's showing me it's that way."

I turned toward the new path.

"Wait," Cianna said. I stopped and glanced at her. "That way? There's nothing there. Just a meadow and a series of caves."

"He showed me the meadow," I said, smiling. "I think the flower is there."

Cianna shook her head. "No, it can't be. I was just there the other day, collecting herbs. There was nothing there."

"Doesn't the flower appear at random locations and out of nowhere?" Ellie asked.

"Good point," I said.

"Yes," Cianna said, sounding annoyed. "How long have you been feeling the call of the flower?"

I swallowed hard, hating to admit that. "Five days."

"Then it can't be. I'm sure I was there not five days ago."

I frowned. "Are you sure? You could have missed it."

"Have you seen the flower? It's huge and bright and it emanates a strong sweet scent. There's no missing it."

This woman was getting on my nerves. "Then your calculations are wrong and you went there more than five days ago."

"I'm sure I did—"

"Look," I said, reigning in my voice before I was harsh to her. "I trust Felix. If he thinks the flower is there, then I think so too."

She shook her head. "This is a mistake. If you go that way, you'll be wasting your time. The flower won't be there and it'll take us even longer to get to Hollow's Bane."

I glanced at my friends. "What do you guys think?"

Theron and Artan shared a tense look. Then Theron turned his eyes to Cianna. "I think that lion is crazy about Mirella and he wouldn't trick her."

"We're gonna follow Felix," Artan added.

I didn't say anything else out loud.

Show me the way, I told Felix.

He let out a low rumble and marched down the path, and the five of us followed. Cianna remained quiet near the back. I wasn't even sure why she was still coming with us. Once we found the flower, would she come back to the enclave with us? If not, then why hadn't she turned around and gone back to her cabin?

I pushed those thoughts away. I didn't have time for them. I was about to find my first heart flower and I couldn't wait. My insides tingled, my hands shook, and my heart raced. Oh, by Saint Sara-la-Kali, I would finally be able to make a ton of heart elixir, cure all the sick tziganes, and pass it along, making sure everyone had a little bit and were stronger and more powerful. Then, I would have time to learn and control more of my powers, and next time the flower showed up, I would be ready. I was sure of it.

In tense silence, we walked for at least two hours. I could hear Ellie's and Theron's and Artan's hushed words behind me, but I ignored them. Whatever they were talking about, it couldn't be more important than finding the flower.

The image of the meadow and the heart animals appeared in my mind ten seconds before the trees opened, revealing ...

The meadow.

With dried grass and fallen leaves.

But no colorful flowers.

No heart animals.

And no heart flower.

I dashed into the wide meadow and looked around, confused.

"Where is it?" I asked in a low voice. I had seen the flower before. Not coming out of the ground, but I had seen it twice —once on my porch steps and another during the awakening ceremony. The flower's stem was long, as long as my arm, and thick, and the center was bright. The meadow wasn't that big. If it was around here, I would have seen it already. My heart sank and I stared at the white lion beside me. "Felix, where is it?"

A picture of the cave appeared in my mind. Felix started walking toward it.

I wondered ... could the flower be inside? Could the flower bloom where there was no sun and no rain? Well, this was a magical flower. Maybe it didn't need all that jazz to grow.

I started after him.

"Mirella," Artan called. "Where are you going?"

I didn't look back at him, at anyone, as I said, "I'm going into the cave."

"The cave?" Ellie asked, her voice squeaking. "A dark, probably humid place? Are you sure?"

I exhaled through my nose. Damn, these people ... they were all getting on my nerves. "You're welcome to stay here and wait."

"As if," Artan practically growled. I heard his heavy foot-falls gaining on me.

"Shit," Theron cursed, before coming after us.

As Felix and I approached the cave, the stone opening seemed bigger and bigger. I stepped through, noticing it was probably as tall as two of me. Or two of Artan. And a lot wider.

A few steps in and the humidity enclosed me. This place was dark, save by the faint light coming from the opening, and stuffy. I hoped I found the flower soon so I could leave it fast.

The cave seemed to go on for a long time. "Lead the way, boy," I said, encouraging Felix.

A low, acknowledging growl rumbled through his throat

and he marched faster, deeper into the cave. Toward the darkness.

"Mirella?" Cianna called. "Are you all in here?"

"Yes," Ellie answered. She turned on a flashlight and pointed at me. "And I see Mi ahead."

"I don't like this place," Cianna said.

Rage course through me and I came to a halt. Damn it. I spun around, intent on asking her why the hell she had come, then. Why the hell had she entered the damn cave? I opened my mouth, but shut it once the ground started trembling.

"What the hell?" Theron asked.

"The opening!" Cianna cried.

The others rushed toward the opening and I stared, frozen in place, as large rocks rolled down over the opening. One by one, they piled up, closing the only way out.

And trapping us inside.

19

SNAPPING FROM MY DAZE, I EXTENDED MY HAND AND CONJURED some of my magic. A small flame appeared over my palm, illuminating much of the wide tunnel.

I still didn't move, and barely dared to breathe, as my friends and Cianna pushed against the rocks. Artan tried to blow them away with his strong winds, Cianna tried to blast them with water, Theron pushed with brute force, and Ellie swallowed hard, probably fighting nervous tears.

Felix lay down at my feet.

"What happened?" I asked him in a low, trembling voice. "What did you do?"

More images invaded my mind. Shadows, dark corners, bright magic, a calling in a different language ... It was like he hadn't been in control of himself. As if his mind had been taken over with dark magic. As if he had been enchanted to bring us—me—here.

And now he was feeling guilty over it.

My stomach sank and I gasped. "Did Muma Padurii do this?"

The others stopped and stared at us.

"You think Muma Padurii enchanted him?" Artan asked.

I shrugged. "I don't know. She did it before. With all of you. Maybe this is another one of her games?"

Cianna let out a long exhale. "It could be. She's known for her devious ways."

Theron grabbed a flashlight from his pack and turned it on. "Now what?"

"We can't move these rocks," Cianna said. "As far as I know, many of these caves are tunnels, all interconnected. We go forward and hope to find some other exit soon."

"If Muma Padurii didn't close them all," Artan said, his tone harsh.

"She can be devious, but she isn't evil," Cianna said. "She would never hurt the heart maiden."

"Right now, I don't believe that," Artan said. He marched to me.

"I'm sorry," I said in a low voice, though I knew everyone could hear me. "He was so sure. I was too ..."

Artan placed a heavy hand on my shoulder, but his voice was still curt when he said, "It's okay. If this was Muma, then it wasn't your fault."

I knew that, but it still didn't make me feel any better. Same went for Felix.

"We shouldn't waste more time than we have to," Theron said, taking the lead. "Let's move."

Theron marched ahead, followed closely by Ellie. Cianna was next, then Artan. I was a few feet behind, feeling like I was taking the weight of the world with me, dragging my feet with each step. Felix was right by my side.

After a minute or so, the tunnel opened into a wide room full of openings, probably to other tunnels.

"What now?" Ellie asked. "Which one?"

"Any," Theron said. "It won't matter. As long as we choose one and keep moving."

He took a first step toward the left most tunnel. The sounds of gravel crunching echoed through the cave and we all stopped, watching the openings with wide eyes. A faint yellow light appeared from one of the openings in the middle and the crunching sound grew louder. The yellow turned into orange.

Soon, the tip of a torch appeared from the opening, followed by an old woman.

She blinked at us. "I thought I heard voices."

We all gaped at the old woman for a moment. She looked even older than Cianna, just as short, but with hunched shoulders and more fragile, as if a strong sneeze would break her. She had long, white hair tied into a loose braid entwined with little blue flowers. She wore a gray and dark blue dress, sandals, and had many bracelets and necklaces and hoops on her ears. Was she a tzigane too?

Artan put his hand on the hilt of his sword. "Who are you?"

The old woman waved him off. "No need for swords, young warrior. I'm here to help."

"You still didn't answer his question," Theron said, tense. His hand wasn't too far from his own sword.

"I'm Mara, dear."

"What are you doing inside the cave tunnels?" Cianna asked.

"I'm a healer, and I have a sick tzigane in my enclave, a few miles south from the base of the mountain," she said. "None of my elixirs are working, so I came into the caves. I know there are some fungi with healing properties that sprout around here, because of the darkness and the humidity. I thought about trying something new with it." She lifted her arm, showing up the small wicker basket looped around her elbow. "Hopefully, it'll work." She tilted her head. "What about you lot?"

"We got trapped in here," I said, but my mind was on the fact that someone was sick in her enclave. None of the normal healing elixirs worked. It could only be the heart disease.

And it was all my fault.

A loud cackle echoed through the cave. "You mean, you're lost. Oh, if you don't know these tunnels, you can get easily lost in here."

We weren't lost. Not yet, but I wouldn't waste my time explaining that to her. "Do you know the way out?"

She nodded. "I do. Come with me."

Mara turned the way she had come and walked away. We followed, but Cianna put her hand on my arm. I halted, looking at her.

"I don't trust this woman," she said, her voice and her eyes the most serious I had seen since we met.

I didn't either. There was something about her that rubbed me the wrong way, but she was our only option right now. "I don't think we have much of a choice here, do you?"

Cianna stared at me for another two seconds, then nodded and dropped her arm.

As we followed Mara through a series of tunnels that went up and down, that were wide and narrow, tall and short, I questioned several times if we were doing the right thing. If we had made the right call in following her out. But I always came back to the same answer I had given Cianna. What other choice did we have? If we went through the tunnels alone, we would end up lost anyway. At least this way we had a small chance of making it out of here.

Hours later—at least, it felt like many hours—Mara announced, "We're almost out."

Three seconds later, light appeared ahead.

I sighed in relief.

As soon we all stepped out of the cave, I tilted my head up and inhaled deeply, rejoicing in the fresh, minty air of the woods. Thank Saint Sara-la-Kali, we were out. And alive. And Muma Padurii was nowhere to be seen.

"Rest for ten minutes," Artan said, taking a water bottle from his pack. "Then we get moving again."

"To where?" Ellie asked.

Artan looked at me. I nodded, then turned my eyes to Cianna. "Will you please take us to Hollow's Bane?"

"Of course," she said without hesitation.

"Hollow's Bane?" Mara asked. "I've heard of that place, but I thought it was only a myth."

Cianna narrowed her eyes at Mara. "Well, it's not."

"What are you all going there for?" Mara asked.

I pondered what to tell her, but she had a sick tzigane in her enclave. Soon, there would be more. If I could find the heart flower and make the elixir, I probably could spare some so she could pass it along to her enclave.

"I'm the heart maiden and I'm trying to find the heart flower."

Theron stiffened beside me, as if he thought telling Mara was a bad idea. Artan and Cianna didn't seem too pleased either.

"You mentioned having a sick tzigane in your enclave," Ellie said, taking the words out of my mouth.

"Yes, and we don't know what it is," Mara said. "I've tried everything I know and nothing works."

"I think ..." I started. "I think it might be the heart sickness."

"From not having the heart elixir in a long time." Mara nodded. "Well ... I haven't seen the sickness before, so I can't be sure, but it might be. We all haven't had a drop of the elixir in years. Maybe over a decade, if not more."

"The sickness has taken over our enclave," I said. My mind went straight to my mother and my heart clenched. "We're after the heart flower so we can make the elixir. If we find it, we can spare some for you."

She grinned, her gray eyes brightening. "That's ... that means a lot. Thank you." She glanced around, visibly touched. "This means I can come with you?"

Trying to act like a nice, diplomat heart maiden, I smiled at the old woman. "Sure."

20

Because of the many wasted hours with Muma Padurii's funny cave joke, we pushed ahead hard, even though it worried me that Mara might break at any time. She seemed resilient, but she still was old.

The sun was halfway down its descent when Cianna announced, "The tunnels underneath the mountain took us too far from Hollow's Bane. I don't think we'll get there anytime soon."

My shoulders sagged. "What do you mean?"

"I mean, let's keep going for a little longer, but then we should consider setting up camp. There's a lake up ahead. That would be a nice place to stop in case anyone wants to bathe."

It was October and we were up in the mountains. With the sun setting, the breeze turned almost too chilly. I doubted anyone would be taking any baths today.

Moreover, the fact that we would have to sleep out where Muma Padurii could easily come and play with us worried me. I wished we could continue through the night.

As I opened my mouth to say as much, Theron beat me to it. "Are you sure we can push it and get there tonight?" he asked.

Cianna shook her head. "I think we're all tired from walking all day, and besides, Hollow's Bane isn't a place to walk into after dark."

"What do you mean?" Artan asked.

"There are narrow passes and booby traps," Cianna said, as if that was explanation enough. "It would be extremely dangerous to attempt to get there at night."

Mara tsked. "Then I think we have no choice."

"Yes, please," Ellie said. "My feet are killing me."

Theron glared at her. "Then you know what to do next time."

She glared back. "And what is that?"

"Don't. Come," he said through gritted teeth.

By Saint Sara-la-Kali. I rushed my steps, trying to put some distance from them and their arguments and my precious ears.

Cianna chuckled. "Are those two always like that?"

"For the last few days, yes," I answered, walking past her.

"I hope his parents are okay with their son marrying a *gadjo*," she said, amused. I halted in my tracks. I had noticed the sparks, the chemistry, but there was still no flirting, no longing gazes. How could she say they would marry? She winked at me. "You'll see."

I imagined how the future would be. Me alone, of course, since the heart maiden wasn't supposed to be touched. Ugh. Artan marrying some beautiful girl who loved him, because why wouldn't she? Theron marrying Ellie. Ha, now that Lovell and Bellville were connected, I wasn't so sure that would happen, at least not while Darcy was head of the elder council and Oscar was *rom baro*. They would never allow it.

Which didn't really make any sense to me, but who I was to argue with millennia-old tradition? It was already too hard to argue about the current problems. I would never win over something so old.

I glanced over my shoulder at Theron and Ellie. Only a couple of months ago, I had learned that Theron had lost his fiancée to alchemists. They would have been married by now. I never noticed his broken heart, only when he told me the summary of the story. Now, as I watched my best friends arguing, I wondered if his heart was healing and finding love again.

Despite everything, I cheered for them. If Theron made Ellie happy and vice versa, I would back their fight against the elder council, if they tried to intervene. I would be there for them and fight with them. The council be damned.

Finally, after a few more minutes, Cianna took us to a flat patch of solid ground a few feet from the lake. She explained that if we followed the water bank to the south, the lake opened in a huge pool, which was always warm—magic from Hollow's Bane—making it ideal for a bath.

Well, when she said warm, my skin started itching and I wondered if I was brave enough to take my clothes off in the woods and go skinny dipping in a lake.

Artan decided to go for a patrol around the area, to make sure it was safe and we were all alone.

"Be careful," I said, afraid Muma Padurii could play a trick on him while he was alone.

He dipped his chin at me. "I will." Then he was off.

Felix went out, probably for a patrol, the opposite way Artan had gone. Theron gathered some wood and put the sticks together in the middle of the camp. I started a fire, while Ellie, Cianna, and Mara went over our food, making sure we rationed enough for later, but didn't starve. Thankfully, we had packed plenty before leaving Cianna's cabin.

Summoning my courage, I grabbed my pack—with my towel and extra clothes—mumbled something about taking a bath, and walked off to the south, along the lake's bank.

Like Cianna had pointed out, the lake opened into a beautiful blue pool surrounded by a white bank and dried grass and leafless trees. It was a gorgeous place, and if the water was really warm, it would be the perfect place for a quick bath to take the sweat and slime off my skin after such a long and disappointing day.

Praying no creepy animal was peeping on me—I chuckled at my ridiculous thought—I placed my towel on the bank, then quickly took off my clothes and ran into the water. I half expected it to be ice cold, but quite the contrary. It was hot. Hot enough to warm me up, but not to burn.

I went in until the crystal blue water was at my shoulders and opened my arms, relaxing. If I weren't naked, I would have lain back and floated in the water, enjoying the peace and quiet.

Instead, I dipped my head, enjoying the peace and quiet from underwater.

When I emerged from the water, Artan stepped out from between the trees.

A ferocious blush invaded my cheeks and I crossed my arms, afraid he could see more of me, even though I was deep in the lake. "Don't tell me you've been there fo—"

"No," he interrupted me. He stayed at a safe distance, close to the trees, and he never looked at me for long, preferring to review the horizon instead. "Hm, I was finishing my patrol and thought about checking the lake, since I was thinking about taking a bath myself." He fixed his eyes on mine. "Is it really warm?"

I smiled. "It is. Really warm, really nice."

"Okay, hm, then I'm gonna go." He pointed toward the camp. "I'll be back later."

"Wait," I shouted. The thought of being here alone creeped me out more than the idea of Artan watching while I took a bath. Actually, the latter brought more heat to my body. "You don't need to leave. I mean, I don't like being here alone, not knowing if Muma Padurii is out there and could mess with us again," I admitted. "If you want, you can stay there." I pointed to my pack on the ground on the other side of the lake. "Just ... turn around."

Without hesitation, Artan marched to the other side of the bank, and sat down beside my things, his back turned to me.

A few minutes went by in silence, the only sound was the water splashing as I washed my body and my hair.

"I can't wait until we have this damn flower and can go home," he said, breaking the silence.

"Me too," I whispered, but I was sure he could hear me. I sighed. "I'm sorry I can't follow the call."

I thought he wouldn't say anything, but the gentleness of his tone when he did surprise me. "It's not your fault. This whole situation has been different. I mean, I don't know, because we haven't had a heart maiden in so long, we can't tell for sure. But, from what we know, enclaves aren't usually divided in two and fighting among themselves, and a heart maiden usually finds out about her powers when she is a little kid. She has time to grow into her powers and learn how to use them." He paused. "The fact that we've been so long without a flower doesn't help."

"It really doesn't." I tried remembering when the last time they found a heart flower by accident was, but I didn't think I knew. So, I asked Artan.

"It was before I was born," he confessed. We've gone out thousands of times, looking for it, but we haven't been lucky."

This topic wasn't helping my mood, so I decided to stay quiet. Until I was ready to get out of the water. After letting Artan know I was ready, I walked out of the lake, praying he didn't turn around by accident. It would have been the most embarrassing moment of my life if he did. I grabbed my towel from the ground and wrapped it around my body.

"I'm decent," I said. "Mostly."

Artan shot to his feet and turned around. Wide, his eyes traveled down my body and then back up slowly, and I felt the prickle of his stare on every inch of my skin, heating me more than the water of the lake. I was aware the towel was small. I had it over my breasts and it barely covered my thighs, but I had thought, well, that it was decent enough for him to see me, at least for a few moments.

He took a sharp inhale and brought his eyes to mine, two golden, molten lava pools that robbed me of my breath.

"Mirella, I ..." He shook his head once, then he took three large steps and invaded my personal space. "I know I shouldn't touch you. I know I shouldn't want you. By my honor, I should stay away from you. But ... I can't resist anymore." He wrapped an arm around my waist and pulled me to him, gluing my body to his.

I gasped, surprised, but pleased. Oh, so pleased.

He hooked his other arm behind my neck, then dipped his face to mine, and captured my mouth with his.

I had thought Phillip's kisses had driven me crazy, but they were nothing compared to Artan's. His lips were soft and warm and silky, and he moved them with purpose. He knew exactly what he was doing and how he was doing it.

I wound my arms around his shoulders and held on tight, clinging to him, afraid this was a dream, that he would disappear or change his mind or leave me alone to pick up the broken pieces.

His hand traveled from my waist down my hips to the edge of the towel. His fingertips grazed my thighs and I hissed as the heat in me built up.

I needed him. I needed him to keep kissing me, to keep touching me, to have me.

All of me.

Decided, I made quick work of undoing the clasp of his belt and the zipper of his vest and pulling them both out. Then, I tugged his shirt free and slipped my hands under, savoring the feel of his hot skin and hard body against my palms.

"By Saint …," he muttered against my lips. He kissed me deeper, faster, harder, then he pulled away.

I stared at him, my eyes wide, even though he still had his arms around me.

"Not this way," he whispered. "Not here."

It was like a bucket of cold water over my head. I stepped back, totally appalled by what I had almost done. Had sex with him in the middle of the woods? In the lake? What about protection? I didn't bring condoms on this trip, and I would bet he hadn't either. And what if someone walked in on us? It wasn't like we were in a bedroom and could lock the door.

Damn it, I was so stupid, letting my emotions get out of

hand like that.

"Hey." Artan put a finger under my chin and forced my gaze to meet his. "What's going on inside that pretty head of yours?"

"I ..." I inhaled deeply. "You're right. This is not the place."

He placed a quick peck on my lips. "We can talk more about that later, okay?" I nodded and he smiled at me. "For now, can you keep watch while I bathe?"

"As long as you keep your back to me while I'm getting dressed." He lifted an eyebrow. "If you're going to see my body—" Heat crept up my cheeks. "—it's not going to be like this either."

He sighed. "Fair enough." He brushed his lips against mine, taking my breath away. Then, he sidestepped me and went in the direction of the lake.

I kept my back turned to him while he took off his clothes, trying and failing not to think that I was naked under this towel and that he was getting naked a couple of feet away from me.

My cheeks flamed and I focused on the browning grass blades underneath my feet, on how dried they felt, on how I wanted that dryness to spread through me and calm my racing heart. The sun was setting and soon it would be cold. Maybe I could lie down on the grass and freeze for a while. That would help. I hoped.

Soon, I had my warrior gear back on—with clean underwear and bra and shirt—and was seated on the grass beside my bag, much like Artan had done before.

My heart and mind raced, remembering his kiss, his touch, his hard body pressed against mine. And the heat was back inside me, scorching me and threatening to burn me alive.

It was too much heat. Heat from my fire, heat from the flower, heat from Artan. I would probably die burned from the inside.

We didn't talk much while he bathed, and he let me know when he was coming out of the water too. I went rigid, once more imagining him without clothes so close to me. More heat crawled under my skin.

"Okay," he said. "You can look."

I stood and turned around.

I stilled.

Artan had his pants on, but nothing else.

I couldn't help but stare at his ripped chest and stomach and shoulders and arms. Holy shit, how many muscles did this man have? I didn't even know there were that many muscles in the human body.

Slowly, he crept up to me. My cheeks flamed as I lifted my gaze to his and found his eyes locked on mine, his stare intense. Deep. Hot.

He loomed over me, halting an inch from me, but not touching me. His breath washed over my lips, and I shivered.

"If this is so wrong, why does it feel so right?" he whispered.

I didn't know what to say. But I didn't have to. Instead, he leaned into me and closed his mouth over mine. His hands snaked around my waist, pulling me toward him, and I melted into him. A happy sigh escaped my throat as I ran my hands over his arms, around his shoulders, down his back.

Holy shit, he was too damn hot.

This wasn't wrong; this couldn't be wrong. Not when his mouth tasted like heaven, and my body curled around his, fitting just right.

Twigs snapped and Artan jumped three feet back. He crouched down, reaching for his sword.

"By Saint Sara-la-Kali," Artan whispered. "You scared the hell out of me."

Felix came out from behind the trees. He projected the image of a quiet, peaceful woods in my mind.

"He just finished going around the campsite twice," I told Artan. "Everything looks normal."

Artan let out a long breath. "It's getting dark and I don't like the idea that Muma is out there, probably watching us and coming up with ways to play with us. We better go back to camp."

A sad feeling weaved through my chest. These last few minutes with Artan had been great. Carefree. Happy. I wasn't ready to go back to the camp and back to this God forsaken mission.

But Artan didn't give me a choice as he adopted his warrior mode and finished getting dressed. Sighing, I picked up my things from the ground.

Side by side, the three of us walked back to camp. We heard their loud, angry voices before we saw the orange glow of the campfire and their shadows looming over it.

"You're just a witch disguised as a tzigane!" Mara yelled.

"And who the hell are you?" Cianna yelled back. "I know the enclave you mentioned, but I don't remember hearing your name before."

We stepped into the camp and found the old women leaned toward each other, brows furrowed, teeth gritted, and hands clenched, as if they were ready for a fist fight.

"You know my enclave?" Mara asked, gasping. "That's a lie. My enclave is small. If you had stopped there, I would have seen you before."

Cianna snorted. "By Saint Sara-la-Kali, you're lying. Everything you say is a lie!"

"What the hell?" I asked, stepping between them. "What's going on here?" The women continued glaring at each other around me. I looked at Theron and Ellie, who were seated at the edge of the camp, eating casually. "Couldn't you two have done something?"

"Oh, we tried," Theron said.

"They almost turned on us," Ellie said.

I looked from Cianna to Mara. "What's going on here?"

Cianna blurted, "You can't trust her. Everything this old hag says is a lie," at the same time Mara yelled, "This old witch is tricking all of you."

"Wait, stop." I let out a deep breath, thinking of how to be diplomatic here. I didn't know either women. I didn't know who to trust. And why the hell couldn't I trust both? Why did one have to be right and the other had to be wrong? I didn't get it. "All right. This is childish. Can we all act like adults and consider there are two or even three sides to everything?"

From above Cianna's head, I saw as Artan cocked an eyebrow at me. I fought not to roll my eyes at him. Yeah, yeah, I knew I acted childish all the time, but that was another story.

"Anything she tells you, it's going to be a lie," Cianna said.

Oh my word, she kept repeating that. I glared at her. "And why should I believe you about anything?"

She pursed her lips and unclenched and clenched her fists. I thought she wouldn't say anything, which would have me concluding she was the one lying.

But then she blurted out words I never expected to hear.

"Because I'm your grandmother!"

I was sure I heard her wrong.

"W-what?" I asked, my voice growing thin.

Cianna's green eyes softened and she tilted her head, staring at me—and that was when I realized my eyes were almost the same shade as hers.

I gasped.

"Marisa is my daughter, and so, you're my granddaughter," she said, as if that was explanation enough.

I took a step back, needing fresh air. Artan was right there, his hand on my back.

"Mirella ..."

I waved Artan off and sank down to the ground, facing the campfire. "Tell me." My voice was barely above a whisper.

Cianna sat down in front of me. "What do you want to know?"

"Everything," I croaked. My mind spun, my heart clenched. "Why didn't you stop my mother from being banished? Why didn't I know of you before? Why do you live alone in the middle of nowhere? Why did Darcy almost have a fit when I said your name?" I pressed two fingers to my temples, feeling a headache coming. "I'm sure more questions will come, but you can start with those."

The others retreated to the edge of the camp, as if they didn't want to interfere with this revelation, but couldn't get away from it either. Even Mara stopped bickering and just watched.

I ignored them all and focused on Cianna.

"Since she was little, your mother had been promised to another tzigane from the Lovell enclave. It was all set and done, as it usually is. But being free spirited and stubborn, Risa, or Marisa as she called herself nowadays, always wanted more. When she was a teenager, she started sneaking off the enclave, and at first, I thought it was to go into town to study or dance. It was only much later that I found out she had met someone and was in love. With a *gadjo*, no less. Thankfully, nothing happened and I was able to explain our traditions and cultures and expectations. She understood, at least I thought she did, and she stopped sneaking out and seemed dedicated into getting to know more about her betrothed. A couple of years later, she announced she was pregnant by a *gadjo*." Cianna's eyes misted over. "It felt like she had stabbed my heart and twisted the dagger. She threw everything we were, all of our traditions, our good name, everything, into the dirt. Oh, her father." She bristled and I gasped. Oh by Saint Sarah-la-Kali, I had a grandfather. "He wanted to kill her."

I frowned as another revelation dawned on me. "Where's he?"

Cianna's shoulders sagged some more. "He died a couple of months after Marisa was banished." She sighed. "He was a warrior, and after her banishment, he was ruthless. He took any mission he could, especially if they were dangerous. He died fighting alchemists. But in truth, I think he died of a broken heart."

I didn't know what to say to that.

Cianna continued, "After your grandfather died, I found myself alone. I started questioning everything. I realized Marisa's banishment was wrong. I armed myself with all kinds of arguments and faced the elder council. I battled them, trying to make them see reason, but it was a one-woman war. I was alone and they were powerful." A tear rolled down her wrinkled face. "I wasn't banished, but I wasn't welcome anymore either. So, I packed and left."

"And you came here?"

"No, not at first. I went after you and your mother."

"W-what?"

"But I didn't find you two. Tracking is not one of my talents, and your mother got really good at staying out of sight."

"She said we had to, because of alchemists."

She nodded. "Yes, which was good for you, but not so good for me. For three years, I searched for the two of you, and I don't think I ever ended up in the same state as you." She smiled and another tear rolled down. "Then, I came here."

"Wait ... how did my mother know where to find you?"

She shrugged. "I really don't know. That's something I intend to ask her, once we find the flower and make the elixir and save her."

That was a question I wanted to ask my mother. I couldn't wait to find this damn flower and go home. We had been out for less than sixty hours and so much craziness had already happened.

"This is crazy," I whispered without meaning to.

"I know it all sounds crazy, but it's the truth, I swear." Her trembling hand reached for me. "From the first time I saw you, I knew there was something about you. Then, you mentioned your mother and that she is sick." Her hand rested on mine and I stilled, not sure if I wanted to welcome her caress or hide from it. More tears spilled from her eyes. "I was so incredibly happy to finally meet you, but my heart is breaking for your mother." She sniffed. "I can't believe she's sick."

And I couldn't believe everything I was hearing. Not yet. "I need time," I said, scooting back. "I need time to process all this."

"Of course, I understand." Cianna wiped her tears and offered me an encouraging smile, one I was sure was hard to conjure right now. "Take all the time you need."

My mind reeled. I didn't need just time; I also needed space.

I shot to my feet. "I ..." I didn't say anything as I turned and walked away.

"Mirella, where you're going?" Artan asked, coming after me.

I lifted my hand to him. "I need a moment alone."

"But it's dark," he said. "You shouldn't go out there alone."

"I won't go far," I said. "Please, give me a minute alone."

I stepped forward and walked into the darkness.

22

I WALKED FOR A DOZEN STEPS AND TOOK A DEEP BREATH. THE scent of the trees and fallen leaves and the warm water of the lake filled my nostrils—followed by the scent of betrayal and loneliness and lies.

Everywhere I looked, people lied to me, omitted things, or manipulated me.

My mother had lied to me, and now, I learned she had known where to find my grandmother and had never told me. She had never reached out to her own mother. Hadn't introduced me to her. Hadn't come to make sure she was okay.

It just didn't make sense ...

Nothing made sense.

Like the fact that I was the damn heart maiden and couldn't follow the call burning in my chest.

It was like opening a can of worms. One bad feeling sneaked out and took hold of me, bringing along ten thousand others. Pure doubt and frustration crawled into my head, filled my heart, and dragged me down.

I needed more time. I needed more space.

I took a few more steps, as if the air could get less stuffy, less cloudy, less lonely the farther I went from camp.

Drowning in my misery, I almost didn't notice how far I had gone until total darkness surrounded me.

Raising my hand in front of me, I conjured a small flame in my palm and looked around. Trees, bushes, roots. Nothing distinct to tell me where I was, or how far I was from camp.

Shit. What had I done?

My misery was replaced by fear, more specifically fear of Muma Padurii.

Shit, shit, shit.

A ruffling sound came from behind me. My heart seized, but I whipped around, ready to blast Muma's ugly face out of here.

"Hey, it's me," Mara said, raising her hands in front of her. She was holding a small torch.

"W-what are you doing here?"

"It has been a while since you left camp. Cianna and I went out to search for you since we know the mountain." She offered me a sympathetic smile. "I'm glad I found you."

"Me too," I confessed with a relieved exhale. "I have no idea where I am. If I tried getting back to camp alone, I would only get more lost, I'm sure."

She beckoned her torch toward the trees. "No time to waste. Let's go."

Without a choice, I held my hand up and followed her.

After a few minutes of silence, I asked, "Hm, what was up between you and Cianna?"

She shrugged. "I don't know. I think ... maybe just two bitter old ladies? She probably thinks she knows the entire mountain; I think I know the entire mountain … I guess stubbornness gets worse with age."

If only it were that, but it wasn't. Since we first met Mara, I had a funny feeling about her. I remembered feeling relieved that she had found us in the cave and led us out, but after that, it was like I had an itch I couldn't scratch.

And the fact that I had learned Cianna was my grandmother didn't come into play.

Nevertheless, I was lost in the mountains in the dark. I was sure I was having second thoughts about Mara because of all the heightened emotions dancing within me. Hell, since I found out I was the heart maiden, or even before … when I found out I was a tzigane.

"How is it?" Mara asked, breaking the silence.

"How is what?"

"To be the first heart maiden after so long?"

My brows furrowed. "Honestly, I don't know. I only recently learned about tziganes. I only learned about heart maidens a few days after I found out I was a tzigane."

"Wow, that must have been scary."

I snorted. "That's one of the emotions I felt." And I still felt now.

She glanced at me. "Want to talk about it?"

I fixed my eyes into the darkness ahead. "There's nothing to talk about. I didn't choose this, it chose me, and there's nothing I can do to change it." She stopped and I had to turn to look at her. "Mara?"

The shadows of fire from the torch danced over the planes of her face, making her wrinkles deeper, her eyebrows bigger, her face creepier. "What if I told you there may be a way to change that?"

My mouth fell open.

I blinked.

"W-what? How?"

One corner of her lips curled up into a wicked smile. "Come with me." She extended her hand to me. "Come with me and I'll show you."

I took a large step back, suddenly afraid of the stranger standing beside me. "What's going on?"

She matched my step, coming toward me. "I have so many secrets to tell you, so many things to share. If you come with me, you'll be the ruler of your own destiny. You'll make your own fate."

If I forgot the fact that she sounded insane, her words resonated with me. I really wanted to know how I could stop being the heart maiden, how I could make my own fate.

I stared at her outstretched hand, wondering for a brief moment, what it would be like if I took it.

I wasn't that stupid, though. Yes, I was hurt and upset and still unsure of so many things about my damn life, but I understood it was my own and no one else's. If it was a burden, then it was mine to bear. There were too many people counting on me, including my friends and my mother.

I wouldn't let them down.

Channeling my magic, I raised my hands and planted my feet on the ground, ready for a fight. "Back off or I'll hurt you."

"You don't—"

A spray of water as thick as a tree's trunk hit Mara from the side, sending her careening in the opposite direction.

"Get away from my granddaughter!" Cianna yelled, stepping to my side. She pushed her hands forward and sent more water toward Mara.

"I'm the only one trying to help her!" Mara screamed,

regaining her footing.

"Right now, you're mad and you'll leave at once!" Cianna sent a new, hard spray of water toward Mara.

"This isn't over!" Sputtering, the old woman was sent farther away.

When the water stopped flowing and Cianna dropped her hands, Mara was gone.

"Where is she?" I asked, looking around.

"If she knows what's best for her, she's gone."

I glanced at Cianna. "Do you know her?"

"No, but I had a bad feeling in here—" She put her hand over her chest. "—since she found us in the cave." Then she turned to me, her eyes a mixture of relief and worry. "Where did you go? Why did you go so far from camp?"

My cheeks flamed. "I ... I wasn't thinking straight. I let my mind and my feet wander."

Cianna sighed. "Have you sorted out your thoughts?"

I didn't want to lie to her. "Not really."

She nodded. "I understand, but it's not safe here. My suggestion is for you to take all the time you need after we get to Hollow's Bane and find the flower."

With Muma Padurii and now crazy Mara on the loose, I wouldn't object. "Sounds like a good plan."

"All right. Let's get back to camp."

It took us almost an hour hiking in the near dark—the only source of light was the flame over my palm—to get back to camp. I was stunned by how far I had gone from camp and hadn't even noticed it at the time.

Once I stepped foot in the bonfire's light, Artan rushed to me.

"By Saint Sara-la-Kali." He reached for me, but stopped short right before touching me. He dropped his arms to his sides, his hands curled into fists, as if he was fighting with himself. I could see it. I knew what was going on "I was going out of my mind here," he whispered so only I could hear him. "Don't ever do that again. Promise me you'll never do that again."

As I guessed, he had been worried about me, but now he didn't want to show just how much that had affected him in front of the others. After all, Artan was made of pure honor. He couldn't have feelings for me.

That hurt more than I wanted to admit. Pretending to be all right, I gave him a smirk. "Don't you know me? I can't promise that."

He shook his head once. "You'll give me a heart attack one of these days."

"You'll survive."

"We'll see," was all he said before he walked to the bonfire, where Theron and Ellie and Cianna were seated. Felix lay beside them, his shining eyes on me. I didn't dare search his mind now.

I stared at his back, wallowing in the hurt snaking into my chest. It was as if he hadn't even kissed me before, as if we hadn't made a silent promised to be together soon. Had I imagined it all?

Ellie cocked an eyebrow at me. My cheeks were probably red from embarrassment and frustration, but I just shook my head slightly, letting her know whatever she had seen and noticed was a little messy right now.

I sat down beside Artan and Cianna, who promptly handed me a paper bowl with cheese, bread, and an apple.

"I brought chocolate, marshmallow, and crackers," she said. "We can make s'mores later as dessert."

"Hm, I love s'mores," Theron said. "I think I'll pass on our fabulous dinner and wait for dessert." He dropped the paper bowl on the ground in front of his legs.

I chuckled.

Dinner was bleak, but it was okay. We had had a hearty breakfast this morning at Cianna's house, and hopefully, we would be on our way home tomorrow night. Soon, everything would be all right.

Trying to enjoy the moment and not think about responsibilities and stakes, I placed the marshmallow between chocolate pieces and crackers at the end of my stick and put it over the bonfire.

The flames shot up, higher than before, and burned my s'mores to a crisp in two seconds.

"What the hell?" I examined my burned dessert.

"That was odd."

The fire shot up again, higher this time. Gasping, we scooted back. Felix snarled at the bonfire.

"What's going on?" Ellie asked, her voice trembling.

"I ... I don't know," Cianna answered.

The flames flashed up again, even higher, going up to the tree branches above us, and a heavy scent surrounded me— the warm, sweet scent of the heart flower.

The warmth that never really left me increased, becoming scorching heat.

My chest burned on the inside and I groaned, doubling over.

"Mirella, what is it?" Artan asked, his hand on my back.

The heat increased some more, but settled and I could feel through it.

I could *feel* ...

Gasping, I finally said the words I had been dreaming about, "I can follow the flower."

23

I BARELY BREATHED RIGHT WHILE RUSHING THROUGH THE woods and around the mountain. I had my hand raised high with a nice sized flame over my palm, but its light did little to prevent me from stumbling over raised roots and stones every few steps.

The ecstasy inside my chest was almost nothing compared to the feeling of the flower that had seized my heart.

By Saint Sara-la-Kali, I felt the damn call and I could follow it. It was like a thin line, a rubber band, tugging and stretching, pulling me toward it. It was so faint and fragile, I was afraid it would disappear or break if I didn't rush.

I tripped over a rock and fell on my knees, putting out the fire in my hand.

"Mirella." Artan was by my side in a flash. He held my elbow and helped me up. "You have to slow down or you'll end up falling off a cliff or something."

"I can't slow down," I said, out of breath. Not because I was tired, but because this feeling consumed me. It drained my energy, channeled my power, and took every ounce of my strength. "I'll lose it if I slow down."

I freed my arm from his grip, conjured another fire in my palm, and kept going.

I heard some whispers from the group behind me, but I didn't care. Right now, all that mattered was the flower. Only the flower. I had to get to the flower.

Suddenly, the line stretched and stretched, more and more. I sprinted forward.

"No, no, no ..." Desperate tears came to my eyes. *Please, Saint Sara-la-Kali, make the line hang on.*

The line stretched some more and snapped.

I gasped as the line ricocheted, cutting through me as if it could draw blood. I halted, lost and weak.

I was about to fall on my knees and weep, but the light from my fire illuminated a small pass, like a rough stone bridge, and Muma Padurii stood on the other side.

"Hello again, heart maiden," she said, her rough voice echoing through the night.

My heart squeezed. "What happened? What did you do?"

"Oh, you mean the call? Don't worry, the flower is right behind me."

I took a step toward the pass. "You aren't going to let me pass, are you?"

Her lips turned into a wicked smile. "I will, but first you have to answer an easy riddle."

"A riddle?"

Artan stepped up to my side. "What game are you playing?"

Theron showed up on my other side. "Let us pass, old hag. We don't have time to play."

"Of course you do," Muma said. "Everyone has time to play. If you don't, then you have to make time for it."

Artan pulled out his sword. "Get out of the way."

Vines shot from the ground and entwined around Artan's legs and arms. His sword clanked on the ground.

"Muma!" I yelled. "Stop this!"

"I will let him go and I'll let you pass once you answer my riddle."

"Don't give in to her, Mirella," Artan said, struggling against the vines.

"This is bullshit," Theron muttered, going for his sword.

I put my hand on his arms. "No, don't."

He froze, but by the hard set of his brows, I knew he didn't like it.

Cianna appeared beside us. "Just answer the riddle, Mirella. It'll be easier than fighting her. Besides, we're just wasting time arguing with her."

I hated giving in to Muma, but Cianna was right. "All right. What's your riddle?"

Muma dragged her feet to the middle of the pass. It was so narrow, I thought if a strong wind blew past, it would take her down. An image of Artan conjuring his air power and knocking Muma down the ravine filled my mind, but I pushed it aside. She was a magical being. She would be back upon us in a second.

"Ready?" she asked. I only nodded, nervous. I was terrible at riddles. "What brings warmth to those who are close, but death to those who draw near?"

A gasp came from behind me. "I know!" Ellie shouted.

"Shush," Muma yelled. "Only the heart maiden can answer it. No help otherwise this pass will collapse and you won't get to the flower."

Shit.

I thought hard about it.

Warmth, close, death, near. The heart flower brought warmth to me, and so far being the heart maiden had brought only despair and death and confusion. Could that be it? I doubted it would be that simple.

I got lost in thought, making a mental list of possible things that could bring death to someone who got too close.

I glanced into the flame in my hand, trying to focus, and it hit me.

"Fire," I blurted out. I slapped my mouth with the other hand. I meant to have thought about it before saying it, but now it was done.

Muma's smile widened. "You're right, heart maiden. Fire, your fire, brings warmth, but it also brings death."

Death is coming for you.

The words of that Romani woman echoed in my ears. It had been months since I had first heard it, but it now made my heart bump faster.

An almost grin over her bark-like lips, Muma winked at me and then she was gone.

Just like that. Like a switch had been flipped, Muma disappeared from the bridge like pass, and the vines were gone from around Artan's limbs.

My hands trembled and my heart took off as I sprinted over the pass, knowing I should have been more careful when crossing something so narrow and precarious. But right now nothing was more important than the flower.

The bridge ended in a line of short trees. Holding my breath, I stepped through them and stood at the edge of a small meadow full of little, white flowers.

Right in the middle was the beautiful, bright heart flower.

But it had been plucked from the ground, and it now rested in Mara's hands.

24

MY friends lined up beside me. ARTAN and THERON with their swords, Cianna and Felix with their magic, and Ellie with her spunk.

"H-how are you holding the heart flower?" I asked, my voice trembling.

"Here's a little secret." Mara smiled at me as orange light surrounded her. Her wrinkled skin smoothed. Her gray hair turned light brown. Her body grew lithe. She transformed from the old woman with gentle eyes into an enchanting young beauty with a wicked grin. "You may know me as Damara."

I had the urge to scratch my ears. I couldn't have heard her right. It didn't make sense. It couldn't be.

"That's impossible," Artan breathed.

"Why? Because I'm supposed to be dead?" Her voice was as sweet as honey.

"You would be over two hundred years old!" Theron exclaimed.

"Don't you know it's not polite to mention a woman's age,"

she said teasingly, but with a threatening layer. "You see, after the council killed the love of my life, I knew I couldn't trust them anymore. I hated them with every fiber of my being. So I faked my death and fled. Since I was the only one able to find the flowers, I've been going after them and feeding on their power—and keeping them to myself."

"That's how you've been young and strong for so long," Cianna said, stunned.

"Exactly," Damara said with a winning smile.

"No, that's impossible," Artan repeated.

Damara cocked an eyebrow at him. "Why is that?"

"Because there can only be one heart maiden at a time," Theron said.

The air fled from my lungs and I felt dizzy. Damara was alive. She was the heart maiden. So ... I wasn't? What was I, then?

My despair was short-lived when Damara snorted. "Another one of the elder council lies. Very rare and difficult, yes. Impossible, no."

I gasped. "T-they lied about that?"

"Dear Mirella, they lie about ninety-nine percent of the things they say. Haven't you figure that out yet?" She shook her head. "It's a shame you won't ever find out for yourself."

Felix growled at Damara. He projected an image of her turning into the old woman again, but this time, she kept aging, until she became dust. Unfortunately, I doubted defeating Damara would be that easy.

"Why is that?" I asked.

Her grin stretched wider. "Because ever since I learned about your existence a couple of weeks ago, I've been planning on how to get to you, so I can steal your powers and kill you." She pushed her hands forward and a spray of fire shot straight at me.

All I could do was stare at it, at the beautiful orange wave coming at me. She had fire. She could summon and control fire. Just like me. Just like a heart maiden. It really was Damara. And she was here to kill me.

Artan knocked me out of the way. "We have to fight," he said. "She'll be strong. Use your magic."

I snapped out of it.

When we straightened, ready for a fight, Damara didn't attack or charge. Instead, she waved the heart flower in her hand, then spun on her heels and ran away.

"Hey," I yelled, running after her.

Not even three steps later, heat licked my back. I glanced over my shoulder at the huge wall of fire Damara had erected, dividing my friends and me.

"Mirella?" Artan called. "What's happening?"

"Damara took off," I said. "I'm gonna try to bring this wall down." Summoning my power, I raised my hands and put all my strength into crumbling the wall. My magic trembled and the wall didn't move an inch. "I-I can't."

She was too damn powerful.

"Wait there," Theron said. "We'll find a way around it and meet you."

By then, Damara would be long gone with the heart flower—the only thing that could save the sick people in the enclave. The only thing that could save my mother.

"I'm sorry," I whispered, sure they didn't hear me.

A pang cut through my heart before I took off, chasing after Damara.

25

———

She was probably going slow on purpose, to let me catch up with her, because in less than a minute, I saw her figure weaving through the trees, going up the mountain. I didn't think twice, I dashed forward. Someone had to chase her and know where she was going, and right now, there was only me.

Finally, I crossed a line of trees and they opened to a wide flat field, and right past it, on the edge of a rocky cliff, stood Damara and the flower.

"What took you so long?" she asked, a hint of laughter in her voice.

"I get it that the council betrayed you two hundred years ago." By Saint Sara-la-Kali, it was hard to compute that the woman standing before me was that old. "But it was so long ago. I'm sure the council has changed, at least the people in it have. The enclaves have changed. They have united again. Or, they are getting there. Why don't you stop for a minute and talk to me? I bet I can make you see things are different and that you can come back with us."

"I don't want to come back with you."

"Then what the hell do you want? You want my powers? My life? Take it. But give the damn flower to my friends and let them take it to the enclave." I meant it. As long as the others lived, as long as my mother got better, I didn't care. Not anymore. "There are sick people there and they need the flower, or they will die."

"I stopped caring about other tziganes two hundred years ago."

"That can't be true. The heart maiden is a kind person, a selfless person. We give everything we have to the people of our enclave." The thoughts had been there, but I had never acknowledged them. It was what everyone had been trying to tell me and I just wouldn't listen. But now that I had said the words out loud, I knew—I felt—it was right.

"That heart maiden died the day the council killed Emilian." She tsked. "You're so naive, wanting to believe in all the good in the world. Let me tell you something. There's no good. There's only evil and how you fight it. The council was evil, *is* evil, and will be evil forever. The things they do, the things they plan, the way they spin the heart maiden's life into their little fingers ... it's pure evil. Don't let them fool you. They aren't working with you. You're the one working for them and once you stop being useful, they will get rid of you."

I gasped. "What's that supposed to mean?"

"What am I saying? You won't live long enough to feel their betrayal."

Damara threw a fire bolt the size of a basketball at me. Thinking of Artan and his many fighting lessons, I dodged it as if it were a blade. I had barely stepped to the side and another bolt was coming my way. I dodged it again. Then another, and another, and another. I kept moving, to the side, zigzagging between the bolts, trying to avoid them while wondering how I could attack her when I could barely deflect her attacks.

She threw three fast bolts, faster than I could move, and the third one brushed over my upper arm, eating away the fabric of my uniform and burning my skin.

I hissed.

Noticing I was injured and slowing, Damara cast a dozen bolts and threw them at me.

My panic took over and I raised a wall of fire in front of me. The bolts exploded against the wall, shaking it.

"Hiding. That's not noble," Damara said, taunting me.

I didn't grace her with an answer. Instead, I reinforced the wall in front of me while I thought. She was too strong for me. How could I take her down? To defeat her, would I have to kill her? I didn't want to kill anyone. I would rather immobilize her, but how?

My wall broke, crumbling in little sizzles to the ground, and Damara stepped right in front of me. Her gray eyes glowed, turning golden-red like two bright embers. "What do you think you're doing? I'm done playing."

She raised her fire-covered hands and closed them into fists. It felt like her hands were around my neck, burning my skin and squeezing the air out of my lungs. She lifted her hand and I moved up, my feet leaving the ground. Choking, I jerked against her invisible grip. But her grasp only tightened.

Damara smiled at me, an evil thing that chilled my bones. "This is fun."

Dark spots danced at the corner of my eyes. Desperation hit me.

I couldn't die like this. I couldn't die right now. Too many people were counting on me.

My mother was counting on me.

Think, Mirella, think.

She wasn't touching me, but she was holding me and she was close enough. I jerked, bringing my legs back and gaining momentum. Then, I pushed them up and forward. My feet landed squarely against her chest. Surprised, Damara flew back several feet and fell on her knees.

Her grip on me was gone, and I landed on the ground hard, hitting my butt and back.

"You, stupid girl," she hissed, getting up.

I groaned and rolled to my knees, trying to stand up.

With a roar, Damara conjured a giant fire wave. It licked the ground, burning the grass to a crisp, and came at me.

Breathing hard, I pushed to my knees and raised my hand. I used the last of my power, the last of my stamina to part the wave. It swept to the sides less than an inch from me, its heat scalding my already bruised skin.

Damara didn't stop though. She conjured a thick spray of fire. It soared at me, but I didn't have anything left. No power, no strength, no air in my lungs. I was done for and Damara knew it.

If I was gonna die, it would be with honor. Chin raised high, I stared at the fire and welcomed it.

"No!" someone screamed. In a flash, Cianna came out from behind the trees and threw herself in front of me. The fire exploded against her chest and sent the two of us to the ground. I hit my head hard and my vision blackened. My mind was slow to catch up.

The images zoomed by and my breathing grew shallow.

The fire coming at me. How ready I was to die. Cianna putting herself in the way.

"No, no, no," I whispered, scooting up to my elbows, careful with Cianna who was on top of me. Her body was heavy and limp. "No, no, no."

I finally sat up and cradled her in my arms. Her chest ... A sob raked through my body as I took in the sizzled cardigan and dress, the huge hole in them, and red and black flesh taking most of her chest and stomach.

"M-my dear," she croaked. My heart lurched. Oh, by Saint Sara-la-Kali, she was alive. She turned her eyes to me, though from their hazy shine, I wasn't sure she could see well. "Listen to me."

"Shhh," I told her. "Save your energy. I'm gonna take you out of here. We'll find you a healer, and you'll be fine."

"No, *puri chey*, don't waste your strength with me." She reached for me, her hand trembling. I took her hand in mine and held tight. "You're more powerful than you know, dear. Believe in yourself and you'll see you can do anything." A tear rolled down her face. "I believe in you."

Her hand let mine go, her head lolled back, and her body became ten times heavier in my arms.

She was gone.

My grandmother was gone.

Tears filled my eyes and a sob ripped through me.

Damara let out a wicked laugh. "Ah, the dear grandmother sacrificed herself to save her beloved granddaughter. That's so sweet. But completely wasted as I will kill you anyway."

Pure, red-hot rage coursed through my veins, and I let out a scream. I let out everything with that scream: my worries, my doubts, my frustration, my fear. With that scream, with the rage that was being released, I summoned my magic. I called upon the well deep inside me. I hadn't had my mother's elixir in a couple of days, and I knew that there was more magic inside me.

I didn't know it was so much.

Gently, I dropped Cianna's body on the ground and rose to my feet, facing Damara.

She was ready, but not for me. Not now.

With her wicked grin, she waved her hand and the same spray of fire from before came for me. And I waved my hand and the string of fire parted, melting away before me.

Damara gawked at me.

And that was when I attacked. I sent a huge fireball for her chest. As expected, she stepped to the side to get away from it, and then the string of fire I had cast while she was distracted slapped her hand, making her drop the flower.

"No!" she yelled, reaching for it.

The string ricocheted, snapping at her hand again and she jumped back. The string recoiled back to me, bringing me the flower.

"Finders keepers," I said as I closed my hand around the heart flower. The magic inside it pulsed into me, and I almost went down to my knees with its force. But I gritted my teeth and endured it, because I wouldn't let Damara see me weak. Never again.

Fuming, she raised both her hands. "As if you had a choice. Once I'm done with you, I'll take the flower back."

"Not if we can help it," Artan shouted, racing to my side. Theron and Ellie and Felix followed him. The five of us stood before Damara, armed and ready.

"This isn't over!" Damara yelled.

A ring of fire appeared around her, and then she was gone.

"What the hell?" Ellie asked, staring at the place Damara had disappeared. "Isn't she like super powerful? Why would she flee?"

I was glad she had fled, though, because even though I knew I would have been able to fight her for longer now, I wasn't so sure I could defeat her. Or kill her.

Besides, my head was somewhere else.

I turned back and knelt beside Cianna's body. "*Puri daj*," I whispered, caressing her face.

"Oh my God, Mi, no." Ellie's voice broke. She knelt beside me and wrapped her arms around me. "I'm so sorry."

Artan and Theron and Felix crouched down close to us. Artan reached for me and entwined his fingers with mine. He squeezed my hand.

Just like that all my strength, all my power, all my stamina, and all my determination were gone. I crumbled into Ellie's arms and cried for the grandmother I had just met and lost.

"WANT SOME TEA?"

I glanced at my mother. She was standing a few steps behind me on the porch, holding two mugs of tea.

"When have I ever said no to tea?"

With an easy smile, she sat down beside and handed me the mug. "True, but I still like to ask."

I sipped from the sweet liquid. It warmed my throat and my core, reminding me that I was home and everything was okay.

Artan, Theron, Ellie, Felix, and I had returned from the mountain a week ago. According to Darcy, if I had taken one more day, my mother and several other tziganes would have been dead. With her superior mien, Darcy explained to me that there was a ritual they performed prior to extracting the flower's powers, but since we were pressed for time, she simply showed me how to do it. I extracted the elixir from the flower, only about a cup of bright green liquid. Then Darcy diluted it in several long glass jars. Tziganes didn't need more than a tiny drop every couple of months. Diluting it with a special brew made it last longer.

"Besides, this is too powerful," she said as we worked. "If a weaker tzigane tries it out without diluting it, their heart might stop."

There was nothing easy about this whole thing.

Since then, I had been helping administer the elixir to the sick tzigane—while Ryane ran after me, trying to treat my wounds. After we made sure they were all cured, we served the elixir to the healthy tziganes, to make sure they wouldn't fall sick anytime soon.

At least now I could feel the flower and follow its call. Next time, it would be fast and easy.

Hopefully.

"I'm proud of you," my mother said, staring at me from over her steaming mug. I knew Theron had told her what happened with Cianna at the mountain, but she and I hadn't really talked since I got back and she had been cured. As usual, she was avoiding me. "I'm really proud of you."

She had come to me, so maybe this time she wouldn't leave if I pressed a little.

"Mom ... how did you know where Cianna was?"

My mother stared at her mug, and I was sure she wouldn't answer me. Finally, she sighed. "I knew I was going to be banished, so I stole a lot of the elixir and hid it. When I was on my own, pregnant with you and just after you were born, I drank more elixir than usual because I wanted to be ready. I wanted to be prepared in case alchemists found us. That way, my senses were really, really enhanced. I sensed whenever she was closing in on us."

I frowned. "Why didn't you let her come to us?"

"Because she hurt me," she said, her voice harsh. Achy. "She was my mother. She was supposed to fight for me, to protect me, and when the council treated me like trash and threw me away, she did nothing. She didn't even look at me. It was as if I shamed her. Like I wasn't her daughter. So I did the same." She paused. "But I allowed my senses to follow her, and I saw when she moved into the mountains. With the extra elixir."

"Do you regret it now?" Now that her mother was gone and they couldn't fix their relationship. I didn't finish my question, because I knew she would get it.

My mother glanced to the sky. It was a beautiful day with bright blue skies and a big golden sun. Shame it was so damn cold. "It hasn't sunk in yet. But I bet that when it does, I will regret it." She grabbed my hand in hers and held on tight. "Which is why I want you to know, everything I did, everything I always do, is because of you, Mirella. I know we don't have a great relationship, I know you don't like me much, after all I hid from you, but I want you to know, it was all for you. To keep you safe. You're everything to me, and I'll always protect you with all I have."

Tears brimmed in my eyes and I rested my head on her shoulder. "I'm sorry I was such a brat growing up."

She chuckled, the act shaking her shoulder and my head. "You really were a pest."

"Mom!"

"But I love you anyway." She rested her chin on the top of my head. "And I always will."

A tear rolled down my eyes as I opened my mouth and said something I hadn't in many, many years, "I love you too."

AFTER CHANGING INTO WORKOUT CLOTHES, I LEFT MY HOUSE and went in the direction of the training grounds, where I was to meet Artan for our first practice session since coming back from the mountain.

Much to my disappointment, Artan and I hadn't had time alone and we hadn't talked about what happened during our mission. My cheeks heated thinking about his kiss. Or kisses, plural, since it had been more than one.

I knew he was still battling the honor thing and the rules thing, after all, I wasn't supposed to be touched.

A bunch of crap.

I just had to be sexier and more persuasive than any other reason he had to keep avoiding me. I didn't mind if we had to keep it hidden, so he wouldn't get in trouble. As long as he kept kissing me like that, I would agree to almost anything.

But I couldn't ignore the little sliver of fear that appeared behind the other feelings. Emilian had been killed by the elder council for loving Damara, and because she loved him back. I doubted Oscar and Darcy would kill Artan—I shuddered—but we couldn't risk it. Whatever we had, it would have to be between the two of us.

My hands shook with anticipation, and I stashed them inside the pockets of my hoodie. *No need to be self-conscious, Mirella. He likes you, you know that.* Still, my body and the nervousness swimming inside it didn't want to listen to me.

I stepped into the main square and slowed down, watching as a group of people huddled beside the fountain. I scanned their faces and only recognized a handful of tziganes —Darcy, Oscar, Artan, Ryane, and Sloan. I didn't know the seven others.

"Ah, there she is!" Darcy boomed, gesturing toward me.

The entire group turned to me and the self-consciousness was back. "Our beloved heart maiden. Mirella, come here, please, dear." Her voice dripped with fake honey, and I felt the urge to barf.

Instead, I put my tail between my legs and walked up to the group, halting between Artan and Sloan. The urge to reach toward Artan, to at least look at him, hit me square in the chest, but I endured it.

"Hi," I said, smiling at the strangers.

"It's an honor to finally meet you," an older man said, bowing to me. He was probably as old as Darcy.

"Mirella, these are our friends from the Karela enclave," Oscar explained. "This is Jaelle, Bersh, Dulcia, Kizzy, and Mihai." Respectively, they looked like grandmother, father, mother, daughter, and son. The young woman looked my age, or a year younger than I was. She was pretty, with light brown curls and an easy smile. She waved at me. "They've come to spend a few days with us."

"That's great," I said, feeling like I was the first lady in some diplomatic event. "I hope you enjoy your time here."

"We definitely will," Bersh said.

Darcy put her hand on Dulcia's shoulder. "Come. I'm preparing a nice supper for us, and I have appetizers to last us all afternoon." She ushered them toward the street that led to her house.

Artan turned to me, his amber eyes anguished. "Mirella …"

Kizzy stepped in closer. "I've heard so much about you. It's so good to finally meet you."

"Thanks?" I asked, not sure what to say to that.

Kizzy laughed and reached for Artan. She knotted her

hands around his elbow. My eyes bugged. "Artan told me you two have training soon, right? Would you mind skipping it today? I haven't seen him in months." She leaned into him, resting her head on his arm. My heart stopped. Artan looked down at the ground. "I missed him."

My throat went dry. "O-okay," I forced out, not really sure what was going on, but sure I wanted to get away from here fast. "I ... hm ... have fun," I blurted.

Tears burning the back of my eyes, I whirled on my heels and marched the way I had come.

"Mirella," Artan called. I didn't stop. I heard his heavy footfalls approaching. "Mirella, wait."

Despite myself, I halted and Artan stopped by my side. "I'm ... I'm sorry."

I flinched, not sure what he should be sorry about. I looked to the fountain and found Kizzy following the group toward Darcy's house. "C-care to explain what's going on? Because I'm lost ..."

Exhaling, he ran a hand through his hair. "Kizzy is my betrothed."

I gasped as pain cut through my heart. "You ... you have a fiancée?"

"Yes."

"W-why didn't I know that?"

He shrugged. "It didn't seem important. At first, we weren't even friends. Then, we were only training together. And then ..." He let out a long breath. "My feelings for you took me by surprise. I wasn't expecting to fall so hard for you." He lifted his hand and I took a step back. His hand fell to his side. "I should have told you before."

"You certainly should have." I glanced at the group

retreating. At the girl walking away with the group. Artan's fiancée.

I couldn't breathe.

"I told her I had to talk to you about rescheduling a new time for practice," he said. "She has no idea that—"

"You don't have to worry about training," I said, interrupting him. Whatever he had to say, I didn't want to hear. "I'll train with Theron from now on."

His brows narrowed. "No, you don't need to do that."

I stared at him, hoping he saw how much he had hurt me stamped in my eyes. "I want to." I jerked my chin toward the convoy leaving the square. "You should go."

Without waiting for his reply, I continued my trek home.

As the distance between us grew, I couldn't fight the pain anymore. Tears spilled from my eyes, and I was sure I would trip on my own feet and face-plant on the stone ground. I didn't care if I did. I was actually hoping to. Maybe if I passed out, then the pain inside me would go away.

I couldn't believe it. I couldn't believe this had happened.

The honor-bound warrior Artan had fooled me. He had betrayed me. Just like I thought he would never do. It hurt more than it had hurt with Phillip, because I had been attracted to Phillip, but it hadn't been into the almost-falling-in-love zone. But with Artan ... I could see myself falling hard for Artan. Hell, I had already fallen hard for Artan.

Until he betrayed me, betrayed my trust.

Who could I trust in this world?

Damara's words about not trusting the elder council rang in my mind, and I shivered.

No one. I couldn't trust anyone.

Feeling alone once more, my heart shriveled and darkened.

CONTINUE READING ABOUT MIRELLA'S ADVENTURES ON *SORROW Bringer*, book 3 of The Fire Heart Chronicles!

Also, don't forget to read *Earth Shaker*, a novella that is best read between books 2 and 3.

THANK YOU

THANK YOU FOR READING *FLAME CASTER*!

Reviews are very important for authors. If you liked my book, please consider leaving a review on your preferred online store or on goodreads, please!

You can get the next two books on the series now:

Earth Shaker (Book 2.5)
Sorrow Bringer (Book 3)

DON'T FORGET TO SIGN UP FOR MY NEWSLETTER TO FIND OUT about new releases, cover reveals, giveaways, and more!

If you want to see exclusive teasers, help me decide on covers, read excerpts, talk about books, etc, join my reader group on Facebook: Juliana's Club!

I have an exclusive novella set in the Rite World that is just for my newsletter subscribers!

Click here to sign-up and receive your book!

THE VAMPIRE HUNT
A Rite World Novella

Norah is a demon hunter, one of the best graduated from the Blackthorn Hunters Academy. When she's sent to investigate a case concerning demons in a small town, she runs into a very arrogant vampire. Her first instinct is to kill him, after all, he's a supernatural and demon hunters are taught to end all evil.

Cain is a vampire prince. Because of his status, he's in charge of making sure humans don't find out about his kind. During a routine investigation, he bumps into a very sexy demon hunter and he wonders what she's doing on his way.

However, the case grows much bigger for Norah and Cain to handle alone. To find the truth and win this battle, the vampire and the demon hunter will have to hunt together—without killing each other.

How well could this end?

ABOUT THE AUTHOR

While USA Today Bestselling Author Juliana Haygert dreams of being Wonder Woman, Buffy, or a blood elf shadow priest, she settles for the less exciting—but equally gratifying—life as a wife, a mother, and an author. She resides in North Carolina and spends her days writing about kick-ass heroines and the heroes who drive them crazy.

Subscribe to her mailing list to receive emails of announcement, events, and other fun stuff related to her writing and her books: www.bit.ly/JuHNL

For more information:
www.julianahaygert.com

facebook.com/julianahaygert

twitter.com/julianahaygert

instagram.com/juliana.haygert

goodreads.com/juliana_haygert

pinterest.com/julianahaygert

bookbub.com/authors/juliana-haygert

ALSO BY JULIANA HAYGERT

To find links and more info, go to:

www.julianahaygert.com/books/

Shorts

Into the Darkest Fire

Standalones

Daughter of Darkness

Rite World: Lightgrove Witches

The Midnight Test (Book 1)

The Midnight Spell (Book 2)

Rite World: Blackthorn Hunters Academy

The Demon Kiss (Book 1)

The Hunter Secret (Book 2)

The Soul Bond (Book 3)

The Shadow Trials (Book 4)

The Infernal Curse (Book 5)

Rite World

The Vampire Heir (Book 1)

The Witch Queen (Book 2)

The Immortal Vow (Book 3)

The Warlock Lord (Book 4)

The Wolf Consort (Book 5)

The Crystal Rose (Book 6)

The Wolf Forsaken (Book 7)

The Fae Bound (Book 8)

The Blood Pact (Book 9)

The Wyth Courts

Winter King (Book 1)

Spring Warrior (Book 2)

Summer Prince (Book 3)

Autumn Rebel (Book 4)

The Fire Heart Chronicles

Heart Seeker (Book 1)

Flame Caster (Book 2)

Sorrow Bringer (Book 3)

Earth Shaker (Novella)

Soul Wanderer (Book 4)

Fate Summoner (Book 5)

War Maiden (Book 6)

The Everlast Series

Destiny Gift (Book 1)

Soul Oath (Book 2)

Cup of Life (Book 3)

Everlasting Circle (Book 4)